# A WEAPON'S JOURNEY

## BY FRANK MARTIN

She fired a single shot with her M4 and the bullet pierced the wall as a scream came from the other side. Breaking their tight formation, Wolf kicked in the apartment's front door and discovered Adam in the living room, leaning against the wall and bleeding from his shoulder. "I see you have new toys."

"Just for you," she replied, her weapon trained directly at his head.

The other two soldiers followed her into the room and Colt smiled as he squeezed the trigger. "Too easy."

Diving over a hail of green gunfire from Colt's weapon, Adam sprung up and kicked Colt straight back into the wall. The injured super-soldier then raced around the room as Wolf opened fire, her shots trailing just a split second behind his movements.

Aiming at a spot ahead of Adam's path, Raptor timed his shot and fired his launcher as Adam passed him by. The grenade round connected directly with the super-soldier and exploded in a green burst, blasting him straight through the wall and down to the street below.

Impressed, Raptor held up the lightweight weapon with a smile on his face. "Damn. Can I use this thing all the time?"

Barely paying attention to the question, Wolf answered him while helping Colt up to his feet. "Stay focused. We still have to finish the job."

Wolf and Colt wasted no time leaving the room, but Raptor trailed behind, confused by her comment. "Finish the job? But I just hit him with a grenade launcher."

# PART I
## ADVENT

"Men heap together the mistakes of their lives and create a monster they call destiny."

John Oliver Hobbes – Philosopher

# 1

Thirteen-year-old Adam Judson sat quietly at his small, plastic kitchen table. Ignoring the steady drip of a leak in the sink behind him, Adam ate his usual breakfast of a burnt piece of toast and a glass of expired orange juice. His bare toes felt rough on top of the contaminated carpet under his feet, but lead paint chips and mold were common in the city's government-controlled apartments, one of which he called home.

Halfway through the meal, the master bedroom door was flung open as Adam's father, hung over and dressed in last night's clothes as usual, barged into the kitchen. "What are you waiting for? Eat your cereal."

Adam kept his head straight and his eyes forward, refusing to look in his father's direction. "I would if the milk wasn't coagulated."

His dad looked at him with a twisted face of confusion. "What the hell does that mean? Just eat it."

He lifted his hand and slapped the back of Adam's head. It hurt, but nothing compared to the real beating Adam was used to getting. And so he ignored the pain as his father moved deeper into the kitchen. "Spoiled piece of shit. I paid money for that crap."

His father then grabbed the box of cereal and started digging into it with his bare hand. "I'm going out early today. Got some business to take care of. Make sure you get your ass to school."

Adam responded with his eyes still glued to the tabletop. "Yes, sir."

He sat perfectly still, pretending to be a statue as his father marched his way out the door and all the way down hall. Once the loud thud of his father's heavy footsteps became too shallow to hear, Adam zoomed out of his seat, snatched his backpack off the floor, and headed out the door himself.

Adam's days weren't much better than his mornings, but that was typical of most everyone in Manhattan these days. After the mid-21st century collapse, when depression and prejudices forced the American government to take control over the lives of its citizens, the entire island was turned into a breeding ground of degradation.

New York City only had one federal school for all of its low-income children, those lucky enough to still have a guardian willing to be responsible for them. Adam hoped wearing his nationally-issued uniform would help him blend in to the overpopulated fortress of a building, but it never did. Lunchtime was filled with harassment from bullies and the classes subjected him to neglect from his underpaid federal teachers.

As usual, Adam arrived back home around five and went straight to his bedroom. The area was not much bigger than a closet. Just enough space to fit a mattress on the floor, which Adam flopped down on top of before instantly falling asleep.

A couple of hours later, Adam's head shot up off his drool-stained sheets, awoken by the apartment door slamming shut. Through his closed bedroom door, Adam could hear his father yelling, the shouts mixed with crashes as the man drunkenly stumbled around the room.

"Where are you, you little shit?"

The bedroom door suddenly burst open, revealing Adam's father standing in the hallway. Out of breath and covered in dirt, a row of sweat dripped off his forehead before wrapping around his eyebrows and down his temples. Fresh blood, bright and still moist, covered his shirt, while a steady stream of it flowed from his shoulder. From experience tending his father's wounds in the past, Adam could tell he was stabbed, but assumed, based on the random splotches dotting the rest of his clothing, that not all of the blood was his father's.

The scenario was a routine one for Adam. However, he sensed something different in his father's expression this time. He usually expected to find nothing but anger in the man's eyes. Now, all Adam could see was fear.

His father leaned forward, placing his hands on either side of the doorframe. "Where's my dinner, boy?"

"There's nothing in the house," said Adam, shaking his head.

His father lifted his hands off the wall ever so slightly, just enough to slam them back down. "Bullshit! There's gotta be something."

Adam shrugged his shoulders. "There's nothing."

Baring his teeth, the man walked over to the mattress and lifted his son up by his shirt. "Then you should have gotten off your ass and got something!"

Adam didn't know exactly what was coming next, but he took a deep breath of anticipation, bracing himself for whatever it might be.

His father threw him off to the side like a doll. After hitting his shoulder hard against the wall, Adam fell behind a dresser and cradled his arm in pain. Adam's father then grabbed the boy by the leg, yanked him upside down, and slapped him across the face. A trickle of blood dripped down from Adam's cheek as he was thrown back onto the mattress and pulled up again by his shirt.

The enraged man cocked his fist back, ready to deliver his hardest blow yet, but stopped when he caught sight of the bleeding gash on his son's face. Frozen in position, ready to strike, Adam's father took several deep, contemplative breaths before finally lowering his cocked fist.

Confused, Adam scrunched his brow, watching as his father released him and guiltily dropped his head down towards his chest and walked towards the door. The grown man then stopped in the hallway and subtly glanced over his shoulder, pausing just short of looking his son in the eye. "For what it's worth, I'm sorry."

# 2

The next morning, Adam woke once more to the sound of the front door slamming shut. Still blurry-eyed and half asleep, his head popped up off the mattress, surprised that the sun had only just begun to rise. "Dad?"

After struggling to get his aching muscles working again, Adam quickly ran to his father's room only to find the bed unmade and an empty dresser drawer on the floor. It wasn't the first time Adam has seen that sight, and he reckoned it probably wouldn't be the last. There were a million different reasons for why his father could've left so suddenly, none of which Adam could do anything about now. So he pushed the nagging thoughts of his father from his mind and got ready for the day.

It was still early morning, yet most would've considered Adam's normal route to school treacherous regardless of the time of day. He would eventually have to take two buses and a subway to reach his destination, but Adam's commute consisted of walking several blocks through one of the most dangerous neighborhoods in the borough. People had hoped that when the government took over, that meant they would be providing more security, but police presence actually dropped in his area. The government provided them cheap necessities such as clothing, education, housing, and food. The rest of their lives was controlled through crime and fear.

Most would go out of their way to avoid this part of town, but after traversing it for so long, Adam had become numb to the danger and oblivious to the sounds of violence echoing along every street.

Passing by an abandoned building, he happened to hear

such noises down an alleyway. Adam usually lowered his head and continued on his way, but this time curiosity urged him to stop and peek around the corner. With his eyes just barely looking into the alley, Adam saw his father lying on the ground while getting kicked by a group of thugs. A man in a suit barked orders at the gang, clearly behind the beating, and Adam instantly recognized him as Don Trello, the owner of a local gas station not far from their apartment.

"You see, Johnny. You screw up one of my jobs and you get the shit kicked out of you. It's simple, really. I don't know how you fail to understand that."

Trello told the men to back off as he knelt next to Adam's father. He then took out a handkerchief and wiped at the blood covering the beaten man's forehead. "Now tell me: why you didn't kill the wife along with her scumbag husband?"

Adam's father spat out a wad of blood onto the ground before answering. "She was pregnant. I'm a desperate man, Mr. Trello, not a child murderer."

Still on a knee, Trello leaned in even closer. "Well, that bitch went to the feds, and we all know what happens if those assholes pick you up."

"I won't say anything. I promise."

"Sorry, buddy. I can't take that chance. So after I'm done with you, me and my boys are gonna pay a little visit to your son. Make sure he doesn't say a peep neither."

Reaching into his jacket, Trello removed a pistol and placed it to the man's temple.

"No! Adam doesn't—"

The mobster pulled the trigger and a wave of blood splashed across his face. Shocked and appalled, Adam watched from around the corner and fought to keep from cringing as his father's body dropped to the ground. Trello then used the same handkerchief to wipe the blood spray from his own face and returned the gun to its place inside his jacket. "Now for the boy."

Trello's command startled Adam, causing the boy to drop his backpack. The sound grabbed Trello's attention and the mobster looked up, confused to find Adam standing dumbstruck in the alleyway's entrance. "Is that him?"

One of the thugs squinted his eyes at Adam before nodding his head. "Yeah, I think so."

A rush of terror kicked Adam's legs into action as he took off running down the street. He could hear Trello's voice yelling behind him. "Well, what are you doing!? Get him!" The gang sprinted out of the alley and began chasing Adam down the street.

The boy ran as fast as he could, pushing his legs harder and harder against the pavement, but no matter how hard he fought, he could sense the men gaining on him. Adam quickly turned his head to see where they were, only to suddenly slam into a person standing in front of him. Adam fell to the ground and looked up to find an old, homeless woman, covered in filth and rags for clothes. Riddled with boils, the grotesque woman's face wrinkled into a hideous smile, but Adam wasn't frightened as he stared up at her from the ground. "Sorry, ma'am."

She nodded while still holding onto the smile. "It's ok, Adam. I've been expecting you."

"Expecting me?" repeated Adam, confused by her comment.

Ignoring his question, she released her smile while bending down to him. "Come. Follow me."

The old woman took his hand and ran down an alley beside them, pulling Adam behind her as they went. "Quick. Hide."

She pushed him forward, and although confused, Adam obliged by crouching down behind a dumpster. From his hidden position, the boy couldn't make out much in the alley, but against the opposite building he could see the woman's silhouette slowly fade as five giant shadows took over the wall.

Suddenly, a loud, unearthly boom filled the air, scaring Adam into closing his eyes and covering his ears. After a moment, he slowly took his hands away but kept his head buried down low. The strange boom was followed by several different crashes of clanging metal and cardboard boxes. Finally more curious than frightened, Adam peeked around the dumpster and saw the old woman standing in the alley, with the five men lying unconscious on the ground around her.

Shocked, confused, yet mostly overjoyed, Adam crawled out from behind the dumpster. "What ... what did you do to them?"

She stood humbly with her hands clasped calmly in front of her. "Don't worry, Adam. You're safe now. I'm here to help you"

Adam rose to his feet while looking at the defeated gangsters. He then turned back to the woman in disbelief. "Are you an angel?"

She smiled while slowly walking towards the boy. "No, child. I'm far from an angel."

As she drew closer, Adam suddenly realized that he should probably be more nervous of this strange woman. "What ... what do you want from me?"

Softly and slowly, she knelt down beside him. "Nothing today, but you have a destiny, Adam, and fate will lead you to it. But for now, you must rest."

He shook his head, refusing the woman's suggestion. "But I don't wanna ..."

Before he could finish though, she placed a hand to Adam's forehead and the boy suddenly fell fast asleep.

# 3

Old and weathered yet ominously designed, the intricately carved wooden walls of St. Maria's Home For Boys intimidated most everyone the first time they saw them, child and adult alike. Part of St. Maria's Church, the Home was built amidst the boom of the industrial revolution, but had since become infamous for neglect and decay.

It was shut down nearly a century ago, along with the city's other privately-run orphanages, but the need for such a place had returned in the immediate aftermath of the collapse. In its sweeping wave of new societal controls, the government had promised housing for all. This included the country's homeless, who were forced into the towering slums Adam called home.

Children, however, needed supervision. They needed structure. Most importantly, they needed discipline. So under government authority, St. Maria's opened again to house, feed, and educate those of the city's youth without a parent or guardian to claim them.

Adam often heard about the place from other kids at school. It was spoken about as a hole one fell into and climbed out of as a shell of one's former self, if in fact one emerged at all.

Now it appeared as if he was about to become its newest resident.

Adam sat alone in the building's front hall, nervously waiting to learn his fate. Behind the front desk, two female school officials, dressed in identically stark, dull grey uniforms, leaned in close to one another and angled their backs to him, hoping to contain their conversation. They failed. The boy heard everything.

"What's his name?"

"Adam Judson. Federal police brought him in this morning. Found him in an alley, near where his father had been killed."

"Did they even look for other relatives before dropping him off?"

"I honestly don't think they care enough to do that anymore. If they ever did at all."

The older of the two women took a deep breath while turning to face their new arrival. "Well, we always have room for one more. Show him around and get him a fresh uniform."

The younger of the two women humbly bowed her head. "Yes, ma'am."

After introducing herself, the official took Adam on a brief tour throughout the building. It lasted far longer than he'd anticipated. Winding and twisting in no pattern or system, the large, looming halls never seemed to end, and everything around him appeared ancient and unkempt. The stained glass windows were so dusty they had all become the same color, and every floorboard creaked so loudly it felt like the entire building was about to shake itself apart.

The official showed Adam the dorm where he would sleep, as well as the recreation center where she assumed he would be spending the majority of his free time. It was really nothing more than a gymnasium with tables and chairs, where nearly a hundred boys, all dressed in a variation of his old school uniform, ran around screaming in youthful pandemonium.

Unsatisfied, Adam turned to the woman as they stood in the doorway. "Do you have a library?"

Tilting her head sideways, she offered him an unexpected smile. "I think you're the first boy to ever ask that. We do have a library. I'll show you."

Their tour continued to the other side of the building, where Adam followed the official into a gigantic brightly-lit room, filled with what seemed to be endless rows of books. After wandering through the aisles in awe, Adam eventually stopped to pull several books from a shelf. He then turned to the official and asked if it was all right if he took them with him. She nodded and showed him back to the recreation room, where Adam sat down in a corner and quietly began to read.

An hour later it was time for dinner. It took the rowdy boys in the recreation center nearly ten minutes to calm down enough to be shuffled into the cafeteria. Adam followed at the back of the line.

After grabbing his food, a chicken patty and canned corn, Adam chose to eat alone, sitting in the middle of the room, surrounded by the loud boys who laughed as they stuffed their faces.

He spent his meal observing those around him. He assessed who was strong and who was smart. He saw who was happy and who was sad. Each kid had a different story, a different personality, and a different life to live. But they all had a single thing in common: Adam went unnoticed by each and every one of them.

Dinner ended at eight, at which point several more officials escorted the children into the old church for a national pledge of allegiance. Adam found the practice strange and ultimately pointless, but understood its necessity in a government controlled society and indulged the watchful officials who demanded he participate.

Afterwards, the boys were taken to their dormitory, a large barrack-like room filled wall to wall with bunks, and told to get ready for bed. It was a relatively mundane and machine-like procedure. There was no fuss or resistance. Everyone did as they were told, Adam included.

Once every boy was tucked firmly under his sheets, an official flicked off the light and shut the door behind her. Not a peep was spoken after that.

Content with the silence, Adam slowly closed his eyes. He tried to drift off to sleep, to finally relax after a strange, traumatizing day, but all he could see was his father's death, replayed over and over again in his mind. The image of the bloody body burned into the back of Adam's eyelids and remained there for the rest of the night, eventually flowing into the boy's dreams.

# 4

It took Adam nearly a year, but he eventually read half the books in the entire library. Fiction, non-fiction, text books, and encyclopedias. If it was on the shelf, Adam was determined to finish it—and he did.

It wasn't easy. That level of dedication forced him into complete solitude. He always used some corner of the recreation room and somehow managed to avoid ever being bothered by the other boys. Adam kept his head out of trouble and his thoughts to himself, never allowing his eyes to stray into someone else's business.

But the year was long and the recreation room's hardwood floor was uncomfortable. One day, Adam felt it was time he upgraded from the usual spot and risked his isolation by moving to a chair tucked in at the nearest table.

At first, Adam was happy with his decision. He sat quietly with his head buried in the book. It was *Stranger in a Strange Land,* a science fiction novel about a human born on Mars who had come to Earth for the first time. Adam related to the story more than he had anticipated.

For nearly an hour he went just as unnoticed as he had in the corner of the room, until a small inflatable ball slowly rolled in his direction. A boy, probably a year or two older than Adam, went to retrieve the ball. Adam never looked up from his book or even noticed the boy was there, but that didn't stop the stranger from realizing that he didn't quite recognize Adam.

The boy waved over his group of friends as he approached Adam with a mischievous smirk. "Hey, man. Whatcha readin'?"

Tilting his head to the side, Adam quickly scanned the boy

up and down, judging him in an instant before returning his own gaze to the page. "A book. Ever hear of it?"

Amused by the sarcasm, the boy's grin spread even wider as he and his cohorts joined Adam at the table. "Ooh. Smart ass. Well, maybe I have. Let me see it."

The boy ripped the book from Adam's hand and haphazardly examined the cover. "Nope. Never heard of it. Looks like crap."

He then carelessly tossed it over his shoulder, turning his attention back to Adam, seated across from him. "You know, I've never seen you around here. You new?"

Adam sat slouched in an unimposing posture with his hands in his lap. "No. I've been here since October."

"Have you been initiated?" asked the boy, eagerly leaning forward onto the table.

Again, Adam didn't move. "Initiated to what?"

"To the club. Everyone is."

"What do you mean?"

The boy then leaned back into his seat, smugly crossing his arms. "Well, first off, I kick your ass."

Adam humbly lowered his head without moving the rest of his body. "I understand."

After slapping the table in excitement, the boy jumped on top of it and threw up his hands, garnering everyone's attention while yelling out over the room. "Ladies and gentlemen. We have an initiation about to take place. If you wish to—"

Adam shot up out of his chair, cutting off the boy's speech by grabbing his legs and pulling them out from under him. The boy fell backward, slamming his head hard against the table. Adam then continued pulling him by his feet all the way to the floor.

The other boys seated around the table stood up to help their friend, but backed away in shock as Adam calmly flipped over his chair onto the boy's head. A thud, the sound of wood smacking into flesh, echoed through the stillness in the room, and Adam then tossed the seat aside as he moved to straddle the boy's body.

Kneeling down on top of the helpless youth, Adam began punching the boy's face, alternating fists in a fluid, graceful motion. His knuckles pounded the flesh dead on, every strike precise and deliberate. With each blow, the boy's face swelled more and more, as blood flowed from the gashes and cuts littering his cheeks and forehead. Tiny shards of teeth and chunks of skin flung up into the air while the other children stood watching the brutal assault in horror, too traumatized to look away.

The beating only lasted several seconds, but by then the damage had been done. Several frantic officials pushed their way through the shocked audience to reach the carnage. One grabbed onto Adam and pulled him out of the room, while the others futilely attempted to stop the flow of blood oozing profusely from the unconscious boy's wounds.

Once they were in the hallway, the official threw Adam down onto a bench and began to scold him while waving a firm finger in his face. He tuned her out, choosing instead to stare out the window across the hall at the people walking down the street. Falling into a daydream, the boy paid little attention to the woman's words until a single sentence finally broke through his trance. "What if he dies, Adam? What if you killed him?!"

The official paused, waiting for an answer she never expected to come, but Adam slowly turned his head to her and smiled for the first time since arriving at St. Maria's.

"Then it's one less mouth the government has to worry about feeding."

# 5

Outside St. Maria's, a compact car pulled up in front the building and idled there for several seconds before finding a parking spot on the side of the street. It wasn't a particularly expensive automobile, but those walking by, unaccustomed to seeing a vehicle so clean and intact, couldn't help but stare.

A young couple in their late twenties stepped out of the car, oblivious or uncaring as to the attention they drew. Even more so than the car, the neighborhood locals were puzzled by the presence of the well-dressed, attractive man and woman, as they walked up St. Maria's front steps and entered the building. Walking through the halls, the couple continued to attract curious eyes from those around them—particularly the woman, whose long, silky blonde hair caused all of the orphan boys to blush at first sight.

All except Adam, who simply looked them both up and down before continuing to stare out the window.

During a brief tour of the building, a pair of federal medics wheeling a stretcher rushed past the couple on their way towards the front door. Lying on the stretcher was a boy wearing an oxygen mask, his face covered in bandages.

Both curious and appalled by the event, the woman turned to the official working as their guide. "What happened?"

Nervous, the official avoided eye contact as she brushed the woman's concern aside. "Just a little accident. Nothing to worry about. Right this way, please."

The couple followed the official into an empty classroom which hadn't been renovated since the building first opened, almost a century ago. They both took a seat in the small wooden chairs positioned by the blackboard and waited as the official exited the room, closing the door behind her.

A short time later, several St. Maria's officials brought a train of boys in for the couple to view, one by one. The meetings never lasted for more than a few minutes, but it took several hours for the couple to examine them all. Once they finished, they walked out of the room. An official was standing outside the door waiting for them and escorted the couple back through the building.

"Is that it?" The man sighed in disappointment. "What a waste of a day."

Continuing to usher them forward, the official expressed her regret, as well. "I'm sorry there weren't any candidates here to your liking. Maybe I could recommend ..."

As she addressed the man, the woman's attention drifted and she spotted Adam sitting in the hall by himself. She leaned over and whispered into the man's ear, who then abruptly stopped walking and changed subjects with the official. "What about that boy? I was told we would be seeing every male fourteen to sixteen years of age."

The official only gave Adam a quick glance, reluctant to look at him for too long. "He's off limits. Federal officers will be by later to pick him up."

Her refusal only further piqued the man's interest. "What did he do?"

Standing her ground, the official firmly shook her head. "I'm really not allowed to discuss Adam's situation. I'm sorry."

The man turned his complete attention to the boy and nodded with a smirk. "Adam, huh? He'll be the last one we see."

Frustrated, the official spoke to the man's back while fighting to keep her voice from rising. "I'm sorry, but I have a protocol to follow. I can't let you see him."

The man turned back around to face the defiant official. "One phone call. That's all it takes, and your protocol becomes whatever I say it is."

Shocked by the ultimatum, the official's jaw dropped as her back stiffened tight. "Are you threatening me?"

"No." The man calmly shook his head. "I'm simply stating

a fact. You might not know who I am, but you know who I work for, and as far as they're concerned, every one of these children are government property to do with as they wish. Now. Introduce me to the boy."

The official took a deep breath before lowering her head and returning the couple to the classroom.

A few minutes later, Adam sat at a desk in the front of the class. Standing by the old teacher's table near the blackboard, the woman and official waited while the man, also standing, flipped through a small manila folder. He scanned each page for a few seconds before moving on to the next. Half way through the file, he left it open on the table and turned to the official, politely asked her to leave the room. At first she refused, but she eventually granted the man's request after he silently stared her down.

Once the door closed behind her, the man finally addressed the boy in front of him, while returning his attention to the folder. "Hello, Adam. My name is Jason and this here is my partner Christine. We're part of a federal careers program to get kids like you out of places like this and working for the government that's already done so much to help you."

Adam was immediately skeptical of the man's story. "You want to give me a job? But I'm just a kid."

Finished with the folder, the man gently flipped it shut and looked up. "Well, the government's not unaware of the future prospects that children in your situation have. Which is to say, you'll probably live off of federal subsidies for the rest of your life. Instead of becoming a burden on the few taxpayers we have left in this country, the government figures it would do better to get some use out of you. Unfortunately, there are only a few spots open in the program and we just can't seem to find a boy who's a good fit."

Adam allowed himself an amused smile. "And you think I might be?"

Jason nodded. "Maybe. According to your file, it seems you've had quite a difficult life. It says your mom died a while ago. You remember her?"

The smile faded from Adam's face before shaking his head. "No. I was too little."

"I'm sorry to hear that." Moving around the desk, Jason left the woman's side to sit in a char across from Adam. "And then you were raised by an alcoholic, abusive father. Even witnessed his murder. That must've been hard. But it says you wouldn't talk to the police about it. Why's that? Were you scared?"

Again shaking his head with a grimace, Adam shrugged his shoulders. "I didn't get a good look at the guy."

The man's eyebrow rose ever so slightly as if he read the lie across Adam's face before deciding to change the subject. "So, Adam, do you like sports?"

Ignoring the question, Adam simply stared at him for several seconds. His silence confused Jason, who looked at the boy strangely. Adam then smiled at the woman still standing by the desk, before turning his attention back to the man. "Who are you?"

Caught off guard by the question, the man did his best to appear offended. "Excuse me?"

Adam asked the question again, this time shifting his gaze back and forth between the couple. "Jason and Christine obviously aren't your real names. Not that I care, but you're not from some career outreach center, either."

Jason titled his head to the side, unsure if he wanted to be curious or confused by the boy's line of reasoning. "I don't understand."

Adam took a deep breath in and held up his head with his elbows on the desk. "Do you know why that official didn't want you to see me today?"

Wiping all expression from his face, Jason straightened his back into the chair. "No. Only that you acted drastically out of character."

Still with head resting in one hand, Adam used the other to motion towards the door with his thumb. "Did you see the kid they took out in a stretcher when you walked in? That's why."

Christine quietly moved up and sat in a seat next to Jason

as he leaned forward, formally clasping his hands on the table. "I'm impressed … but that doesn't explain why you think we aren't who we say we are?"

Returning his hands back down to his sides, Adam straightened up in his seat. "You don't grow up the way I have without learning to read people. Body language. Facial expressions. Word choice. They all could mean the difference between life and death. A lot can be told from the way a person moves, and you, my friend, are an open book."

Jason fought and failed to conceal a smile. "Where did a boy your age learn to talk like that?"

"The federal school system."

Clapping lightly, Jason let out a restrained chuckle while glancing over to his partner. She still remained silent, but gave him a curt nod. Jason then turned back to face Adam with a reserved smirk. "We are representatives of a government project that will train you for a job. We didn't lie about that."

"What kind of job?" asked Adam curiously.

Jason answered with a blank expression. "Soldiering."

Adam giggled in response, the first time in years that he truly allowed himself to let go. It had been so long he thought he might've forgotten, but the laughter flowed without a care in the world.

"That's hilarious."

This time it was the man who didn't share in the joke. He coldly stared back at Adam and extended both arms out to his sides, offering himself to be judged. "You say you can read people, Adam. Well then you should know if I'm making it up."

As Adam continued to laugh, he locked into the man's firm, unshakable eyes and the chuckles slowly came to a complete stop. The boy then took in a deep, sobering breath and accepted the truth. "I assume since you're telling me this, then I don't have much of a choice in the matter."

Ignoring the boy's comment, Jason formed another smirk before moving towards the door. "I'll go start the car."

# 6

Less than twenty minutes later, Adam sat in the back seat as the car zoomed north up the highway. The journey out of the city had mainly been quiet so far, with Adam enamored by the view out the window, gazing across the massive Hudson River.

He was particularly awestruck by the tall palisades on the opposite shore, which did not go unnoticed by Christine in the passenger seat. After turning her head slightly to catch sight of Adam in deep thought, the woman looked back over shoulder to grab the boy's attention. "Hey."

"So she does speak," said Adam, sarcastically surprised.

Christine smiled, her face filled with laughter. "You seem like a very smart boy, Adam, but you went with us solely based on our word. Wouldn't you want proof we are who we say we are? For all you know, we could be kidnappers, or axe murderers, or members of a crazy cult."

Adam smiled back as he played along. "Well, you seem like a very smart lady, Christine. And you know, it's possible I could've killed that boy today. So I wasn't too keen on sticking around. Kidnappers, axe murderers, and yes, even crazy cult members. I really don't care who you are, or even who you work for, as long as it got me out of there."

Impressed by his logic, Christine's eyebrows rose as she nodded her head. "Good point."

Adam then turned to look back out the window. "Besides, like the man said, I knew you were telling the truth."

"How?" she asked, with her body still turned around.

"I paid attention. His voice, pupils, and breathing were all different between the two stories he gave me. One was a lie and one was a truth. It wasn't that hard to figure out which was which."

Impressed again, Christine flashed him another smile. "How's a boy your age so smart?"

"I read a lot," said Adam, shrugging his shoulders. "And humans aren't really all that hard to understand once you know the little things."

"You speak about humans like you aren't one," observed Christine.

Adam answered as his eyes followed the crashing waves in the River below. "Well, I've seen humanity at its worst. It's not something I want to be associated with."

Christine giggled to herself while leaning over to whisper in the man's ear. Still looking out the window, Adam saw her out the corner of his eye and curiously interrupted. "What is it?"

Not in any rush, Christine finished whispering in the driver's ear before returning her back to the passenger seat. "You're really cocky for a boy your age, when the truth is, you know nothing."

Adam didn't respond to her comment, and his silence caused her to go on. "It's cute, really. You think in your fourteen years of life you've seen humanity at its worst? Then I'm sorry, honey, but you aren't ready for this job."

Without putting much thought into the veracity of her assessment, Adam immediately saw it as a challenge. "How 'bout a pizza says you're wrong?"

Christine turned around once more to look at Adam between the two front seats. "You want to make a bet with me on whether or not you can be trained into a soldier?"

"Yeah," he answered, confidently crossing his arms. "And make it a pepperoni."

Christine smiled and stuck her hand out to accept his offer. "Deal."

The rest of the ride was made in complete silence. About an hour after leaving St. Maria's, the car pulled into a small airport, passing by security with nothing more than a wave, and stopped in front of a closed airplane hangar.

Adam looked around, confused, and saw no personnel present to assist them. "The airport? Where're we going?"

In the front seat, the man and woman ignored his questions, proceeding to talk softly between themselves. Annoyed, Adam gave them a quick wave to grab their attention. "Hey. What's the big secret?"

They continued to carry on their conversation as if the boy wasn't even there. Adam didn't stop trying, though. "Christine, come on. Just tell me. And what about you, Jason? I think I deserve to know what's going on."

Jason quickly turned around from the driver's seat and raised a gun in Adam's direction. "Actually, you don't."

He quickly pulled the trigger and a dart shot straight into the boy's neck before he could even react. Adam felt a slight pinch and winced before pulling the barb from his skin. It was tiny. No bigger than a bee. But its design wasn't what confused Adam.

He looked up at Jason, understandably annoyed that the man had just shot him. "What the hell is your ..."

Before he could finish his thought, Adam's eyes suddenly grew heavy and fell shut, as his body dropped to the seat beside him.

# 7

When Adam's eyes fluttered open again, he was met by the sight of a Hispanic man leaning directly over him. "Morning, sunshine."

The man then turned and walked away, yelling like a drill sergeant. "Let's-go. Let's-go. Let's-go. Time is priceless, children. Wake your asses up. Let's go!"

Confused, Adam sat up and looked around. He had no idea where he was, but the room reminded him of the dorm back at St. Maria's. Only here, the word *barracks* seemed more appropriate. It was stark and metallic. The atmosphere was cold, both literally and figuratively. And he wasn't alone. His bed was lined in a row against a wall with those of ten other kids his age, looking just as perplexed and startled as he was.

The Hispanic man stopped and looked around, annoyed that none of the children had risen to their feet. "Today!"

They all jumped out of bed, but their tired and exhausted bodies struggled to respond as fast they wanted them to. At the front of their beds, the children did their best to stand at attention, with their legs straight and arms by their sides. While freezing in place, Adam rolled his eyes to look around the room without moving his head. He couldn't find any windows, realizing the room was poorly lit by a couple of faint incandescent bulbs hanging from the ceiling. He also noticed a single door at the far end of the room, next to a pane of one-way glass.

With all the children standing before him, the man began strolling up and down the line while continuing to bellow his voice throughout the small, tightly-enclosed room. "Hello. My name is Major Chris Martinez. I will be your lead instructor during your stay in our wonderful facility. Officially, its designation is Site-24X. But for those that call this place home, we just refer to it as The Armory.

"Now, children, I'm sure based on your recruitment that you think you have an idea as to why you're here. Well, you're wrong. You are not here to be trained. You are here as research. Yes, we will train you for combat. You will become soldiers. Very good ones, in fact. But that is not your purpose. That is not our ultimate goal.

"You're here to learn how to fight, how to survive, and how to kill, so that we may apply that knowledge in the training of future soldiers. You are just data. An experiment. And by no means do we give a shit about your lives. You are all easily replaceable. Now, stay at attention. I'll be right back."

The Major continued walking past the end of the row of children and straight through the door at the front of the room. As the door closed behind him, Adam's eyes followed the Major as he took a sharp turn into a room on the other side of the one-way glass.

Upon entering the room, Major Martinez walked by two armed guards garbed in generic military fatigues. He then caught sight of a fifty-year old man, clean-shaven and in a plain dark suit, standing behind the glass and looking out at the ten children. The man slowly sipped his coffee from a porcelain cup and saucer as twenty men and woman sat behind him in rows, typing away on their computers.

Major Martinez walked up next to the man and also gazed through the window, waiting alongside him. Silence stood between them for several seconds until the man finished his sip of coffee and began the conversation. "What do you think, Martinez? Will this work?"

"I don't know," answered the Major, unconvinced, shaking his head. "They're so young. This seems wrong."

The man gently returned the cup to the saucer he held in his other hand. "Well, we've been funded to run six projects, and we had five. This is just to fill the sixth spot."

Restraining his frustration, Martinez turned to face the

man. "But this is the best we could come up with? Giving kids a workout?"

The man shook his head with their eyes still locked through the glass. "Sixteen isn't so young anymore."

"Actually, only six of them are sixteen. Three are fifteen and one boy is fourteen."

In a burst of rage, the man in the suit suddenly flung the cup and saucer to one side, splattering coffee against the wall. "Fourteen!? Who recruited him?"

Neither Martinez nor the men and women working at the back of the room reacted to the man's abrupt shift of demeanor. The Major simply answered his question. "Jason and Christine."

"Get him up here," ordered the man while returning his eyes straight ahead.

Martinez looked back and whistled at the men and women typing away on their keyboards. Understanding the signal, Jason stood and approached where they stood by the glass. "Sir?"

The man in the suit kept his eyes facing forward. "You put a fourteen-year-old in the program?"

Jason nodded, completely unafraid to justify his answer. "Yes, sir, but—"

"No," interrupted the man, turning to face him. "I don't want excuses. He's *fourteen*."

Jason pointed towards the window at no one in particular. "Go talk to him, sir. He's perfect. There's something about the kid that—"

"How can we teach a boy to use a blade to kill when he hasn't even learned to shave with one yet?"

"He already has."

The man turned to Jason, his eyes wide and intrigued. "Excuse me?"

"He got into a fight right before we met him, and Christine just got word this morning that the other boy died in the hospital."

The man looked back through the glass and rubbed his chin with a veiled smirk. "So we already have a killer among the bunch. Interesting. Test him, Martinez."

The Major nodded slowly. "Yes, sir."

The man then turned and placed a hand on Martinez's shoulder. "But first get some rest. You look like you haven't slept in days."

Martinez nodded, turned, and walked straight out of the room. Once he was gone, Jason approached the glass, clearly deep in thought, and then turned to the other man.

"But, sir, what about the children? You're just going to leave them like that?"

The man glanced over at the glass as well, and thought for a second before waving over one of the armed guards standing at the door.

"Sir?" said the guard as he approached.

The man motioned while giving the eager guard his orders. "I want you to stand here and look through this glass. It's not bulletproof. If one of those kids moves, shoot them in the leg."

"Yes, sir," the man replied with a nod, before turning to watch the children.

The man then made a move towards the door, but Jason quickly jumped in front of his path.

"I'm sorry, sir, but I don't understand the point of that. If one of those kids dies, just one, then the whole project is compromised. We need to—"

"We don't need to do anything," interrupted the man, cutting Jason off for the third time. "These kids are the lowest thing on my priority list, right below washing my car. This program might be your whole life right now, but it's just a speck of mine. So next time you want someone to care about these kids, call a social worker. They're nothing to me."

Jason was stunned, allowing the man to easily move him aside as he continued exiting the room.

Six hours later, Martinez walked back into the room and found that all the men and women working at their desks had left. The room was empty except for the lone guard, still watching the silent children through the glass.

Martinez approached the guard and placed a hand on his shoulder, dismissing him, before looking through the glass himself. He waited a moment, allowing his eyes a chance to scan each and every one of the children through the glass, and then walked back into the barracks.

None of the young eyes turned to look at Martinez as he entered the room. Their heads remained staring ahead, steadfast, strong, and without the slightest hint of fatigue, even as the Major began slowly walking up and down the line. "I'm impressed. Some adults can't do what you just did. Already I can see that our scouts made some very good decisions. But this is the nicest I'm gonna be during your stay here, so don't get used to it."

Martinez suddenly stopped his march and out of nowhere, abruptly turned to Adam, before angrily charging straight at him. "What the hell was that, boy?!"

Fighting the curious urge to glance sideways, the other children squirmed ever so slightly, but Adam knew perfectly well that he hadn't moved a muscle. Still, he respectfully answered the question. "What was what, Major?"

Martinez inched his face forward, so close Adam could feel him spit as he talked. "Did you really just do what I thought you did?"

"What did you think I did?" Adam asked again, while keeping his body perfectly in line.

"Don't play games with me, you little shit!"

Realizing their little interaction only had one possible outcome, Adam curled the corners of his mouth into a small yet obvious smirk. "I just thought you would like to play a game with someone new. Give you a chance to stop playing with yourself."

The rest of the children couldn't stop themselves from smirking, but their brief expressions snapped back to attention when Martinez backhanded Adam across the face. After the smack, Adam turned back to Martinez and stared him down, as a trickle of blood ran down his cheek. "Is that it? My drunk of a father hit harder, and he could barely stand half the time."

The comment was meant to get under Martinez's skin, and he knew it. As did everyone else in the room. It failed, though. The Major stared back at the boy, unimpressed by his wit. "We could send you back to him."

"No. You can't," said Adam, shaking his head. "He's dead."

"I know," responded Martinez, nodding once. "That's what I meant."

Finally giving up his at-attention stance, Adam's back slumped as he took in a long, deep breath. "I think I'll pass. But if you really want to arrange a family reunion in hell, why don't you take that gun and plan one for yourself?"

Any expectation Martinez had about their encounter was instantly lost. He'd prepared himself for smartasses. He was ready to take everything these kids had, and more. But Adam wasn't being sarcastic. He didn't sound rude or attempt to be offensive. He simply spoke as if he were asking the Major a genuine question, as if he saw straight into his past and poked it with a stick.

Grinding his teeth together to contain the rising rage, Martinez could feel the composure within him snap. In one swift move, he removed the gun from his holster, tripped Adam to the floor and pointed the barrel directly into the center of the boy's forehead. The two locked eyes and fear finally drove the children around them to watch.

Swallowing deeply, Adam calmly stared back at Martinez. The boy's face was still and peaceful. By contrast, the Major appeared completely lost to emotion as he clutched the trigger with a shaky finger.

After several seconds, Martinez's anger finally broke, and he slowly lowered his gun. He then stood back up, struggling to look at the children gathered around. "All of you, there's a trunk at the foot of the bed you slept in. Get changed into sweats. You have calisthenics in ten minutes."

Barely turning his head, Martinez took one last look at Adam, still lying on the floor, and walked out of the room.

# 8

Tired, sore, and desperately hungry, Adam and the other nine children limped their way into a cafeteria filled with men and women dressed like office workers. Dressed in generic sweats and drenched in perspiration, the kids stuck out from everyone else in the room, but no one bothered to notice them as they entered.

Martinez followed in behind the train of exhausted children and pointed them over to a serving line for food, as well as at an empty table in the corner. Trudging forward like zombies, the children marched in silence to pick up trays and follow the line for food.

Adam was surprised to discover they were actually being served a real meal. There were fruits and vegetables as well as an assortment of lean, unprocessed meats. He had never seen what most would consider a nutritious meal before in his life, but he couldn't imagine it looking much different than what he was being given here.

One by one, the famished children all sat down at their designated table in the corner and began to eat. No one said a word during the feast. They were all too busy ravenously stuffing their faces to speak.

After twenty minutes, the gorging began to slow down and a boy with a Southern accent was the first to speak. "Wow. I never knew food could actually taste this good."

The group remained silent, choosing to quietly pick at their plates rather than carry on the conversation, but that didn't stop the same boy from trying to lighten the mood. "Hey, what's with this place and windows? Are we underground or something?"

Seated across from him, Adam answered without lifting his eyes off his tray. "We might be, but that's not why there aren't any windows. It's a form of control. With sunlight, we would know what time of day it was. If it were night out, we would want to rest. Instead, they tell us when it's time to sleep."

"Wow," said the boy sarcastically. "What are you? Some kind of genius kid?"

Adam still kept his eyes lowered to his tray. "Only on the weekends."

The group lightly laughed as they continued eating. All except for the boy, who continued to stare at Adam seated across from him. "But without the sun, then how would you know?"

Adam looked up at and gave the boy a smile. "Good call."

Smiling back at him, the boy extended his hand over the table. "The name's Travis Sky."

Adam accepted the handshake, while introducing himself as well. The two boys continued talking and it wasn't long before everyone at the table had joined into their conversation.

In the opposite corner of the cafeteria, Martinez leaned against the wall, waiting patiently as the man in the suit approached. He crossed his arms upon reaching the Major. "I saw the video tape of the barracks, Martinez. I told you to test the boy, not put a bullet in his head."

Continuing to lean his shoulder against the wall, Martinez shook his head with an uncomfortable grimace. "There's something not right with him."

"What do you mean?" the man asked, curiously.

"I've killed a lot of men up close, hardened soldiers who weren't afraid to die, and even they couldn't stop themselves from staring down a barrel when it was aimed at their heads. But this kid … He didn't look at the barrel at all. He stared right through my eyes the entire time. As if the gun weren't even there."

"Would you have shot him?" asked the man.

Annoyed by the question, Martinez pushed off the wall to stand tall. "What do you think I am?"

"Just answer the question, Major."

Martinez shook his head sternly. "No."

The man relaxed his arms and placed his hands into his pockets. "You went in there to size the boy up, and he sized you up instead."

Martinez sighed deeply, reluctantly affirming the man's assessment.

When the Major offered no objection, the man smirked while rubbing his chin. "Hm. Seems the analyst was right about the boy after all. He is something special. He saw right through you and now he knows his senior drill instructor is all talk."

"All talk? I put a gun to his head."

"But couldn't kill him," the man pointed out. "And I get the feeling death is all this boy thinks about."

Martinez scrunched his brow, surprised by the comment. "Why do you think that?"

The man turned to look out over the cafeteria as he spoke. "The way you said he stared through your eyes while you held his life in your hands. I've only heard one other person described that way. Stryker."

The Major's confusion slowly fell into disbelief. "I ... didn't know that."

"Well, did you know you didn't work those little bastards hard enough?" The man lifted his chin, gesturing across the room. "They're getting a little too friendly over there."

Martinez turned and immediately spotted the children laughing and joking as if they'd known each other their whole lives.

"Shit," Martinez cursed before storming across the cafeteria.

Every table he passed held workers eating calmly and talking quietly amongst themselves, but the kids in his sight were boisterous and rowdy. They were the only group loud enough to fill the room with commotion, and Martinez only added to it by grabbing the long table and flipping it straight over. "Did I tell you this was a social event?!"

The children all instantly fell silent and stared up at their angry instructor, while the rest of the room continued to eat, unphased by the disruption. Scowling over the kids, Martinez's chest rose and fell with heavy breaths. The tense moment lasted several seconds until the Major eerily calmed himself and smiled. "Follow me."

Upon returning to the barracks, Martinez ordered the children to fall back in line, and he began marching up and down in front of them. "Listen up, because I'm only going to say this once. None of you are here to have fun. You're here to be subjects. Every move you make is studied and you're always being watched. Those people that were sent to find you, they're your analysts. You might see them from time to time, but they're not your friends. *I'm* not your friend. And you certainly are not friends with each other. You're squad mates. Nothing more."

Martinez stopped in the middle of the room and pointed towards the child standing at the first bed. "You. The girl at the front of the line. State your name and where you're from."

The girl stepped up and spoke in a disciplined, monotone voice with her eyes remaining straight ahead. "Sarah Eden. Los Angeles, California."

She returned back to her spot and Martinez then pointed to the kid standing beside her. "Next."

The boy Adam had befriended in the cafeteria stepped forward and followed the girl's lead. "Travis Sky. Houston, Texas."

"Next," bellowed the Major, moving the introductions along.

Once all ten of the children had their turn, Martinez resumed his march up and down the line. "Good. Now that we got that out of our system, I want you to forget it. Your past means nothing. Your names mean nothing. Who you were before no longer exists. So I will give you new names. This is how you will know and refer to your fellow teammates."

Stopping again in the middle of the room, Martinez pointed back to the first child who'd spoken and went down the line, issuing their new codenames. "Girl in the front, you're Wolf. Standing beside her is Fox. After that we have the loudmouth who almost got his head blown off. For you, son, I feel Lion would be appropriate. Next to him, we'll call you Toad."

Disappointed, the boy he'd assigned the name to put his hands up to halt the process. "Wait. Toad?"

"Would you rather me call you shit stain?" asked Martinez, genuinely offering him an alternative.

"No, sir," responded the boy, hiding his dejection. "Toad sounds great."

Martinez then continued down the line. The remaining three girls were given the names Hawk, Tiger, and Falcon while the rest of the boys received Ox, Hound, and Colt.

Once that was finished, the Major turned and walked towards the room's only exit. "All right. Now that that's done, it's time for our second PT of the day. So move it."

Martinez pushed the door open and stood beside it as his troops marched in single file back to the gym.

# 9

As the days passed, the children engaged in nothing but physical training. *Workouts. Obstacle courses. Runs that lasted for miles.* Anything the Major could think of to strengthen their bodies and, by extension, their resolve.

After two months, or at least what the children assumed were months, Martinez began to change up their routine.

He brought the kids into a dull room, covered floor-to-ceiling in grey paint. Small chairs with tables were set up in rows and a white board hung against the front wall. Even with its bland, almost depressing atmosphere, the children felt like they were in school as they took their seats.

That all changed when the Major placed a .45 caliber handgun on top of the front desk. "Congratulations. You've all lasted this long. Now it's time to learn."

Adam civilly raised his hand and Martinez called on him with the same respect. "Yes, Lion?"

"Why are we learning in a classroom and not somewhere more hands on?"

Martinez left the front desk to casually stroll between the chairs. "Because we're going to take our time. Basic training for soldiers is usually completed in months, to get them out in the field, but since you aren't needed anywhere, we're teaching you in years. Everything will be covered down to the tiniest detail. You're not being trained as infantrymen, but as an advanced combat special forces unit. Nothing will be left to chance."

Every day, the Major held one class session instead of one of their workouts. He taught them about weapons, military strategy, the human anatomy, and any other information that could aid them in battle. Several weeks later, Martinez replaced another workout with a shooting session.

After a while, the children began to fall into a routine. Every day was the same. *Workout. Learn. Eat. Shoot.* Nothing changed. There were no exceptions.

Their schedule was a grueling one, but the children found comfort in the repetition. Each day they grew stronger, faster, smarter.

Training had become their sole purpose in life. It was the only goal they lived for. Not once did they ask how their newfound skills and knowledge would be used, or why. But that was all about to change.

Breaking their normal agenda for the first time in months, the Major brought the squad through a small door that opened into a giant warehouse filled with a natural-seeming forested valley. The room, packed with trees, rivers, hills, and more, seemed never-ending. The only hint that they were inside was the industrial-looking ceiling high above and the bright florescent lights hanging below it, a poor substitute for the sun.

After closing the door behind him, Martinez allowed the awestruck kids to break file and wander around, staring at the man-made environment in wonder. "Impressive, huh? The room was designed that way. We can turn this space into any scenario we need to train you for battle. This is our forest simulation."

He then clapped his hands together and took a step forward ready to work. "All right. That's enough looking around. Fall in."

The ten children instantly snapped into a line and Martinez strutted by them. "For this exercise you will be divided into two groups of five. The teams are Toad, Falcon, Hound, Ox, and Fox on Blue, versus Hawk, Tiger, Colt, Wolf, and Lion on Red."

Martinez stopped in the middle of the line and stood tall with his hands clasped behind his back. "We don't want you to kill each other, so the guns are modified to hold tranquilizer darts. One shot and you'll be out for hours. And don't get cute and shoot yourself for a nap. Cameras are everywhere, so we'll be watching."

Stepping out of character, Martinez relaxed his shoulders and brought his arms around to soften his tone. "Now, I want you to use what you've learned and apply it here. This exercise is a battlefield simulation only. Nothing more. It's your first of many, so don't worry about it. It means nothing."

He then took a step to the side while waving the children to follow him. "Red team, come with me. Blue team, your equipment is over there."

Martinez took a single step, then Toad raised his hand. "But sir, how do we win?"

"Simple," answered the Major. "Eliminate your opponent until there's no one left standing ... unconscious of course."

He then continued on his way into the forest with Red team following behind him.

After showing Red team their starting location, Martinez entered the facility's control center. It was a larger version of the room outside the children's barracks, with all their analysts set up to watch a huge wall filled with monitors.

Martinez walked to the back of the room, where the man in the suit did not appear happy to greet him. "Major, explain to me why I must be here?"

Martinez stopped and turned to stare out at the monitors alongside him. "I've done nothing but train these kids for months, in a project you're supervising. This is their first time on a battlefield and the least you can do is watch."

"This better be quick," sighed the man.

Adam reached down and removed a silenced M9 pistol from one of the several equipment containers lined up on the dirt floor. "Simple strategy, guys. Take out the leader."

"Who will be the leader?" asked the girl known as Tiger.

He answered her while carefully examining the weapon. "Fox."

Curious, Tiger asked a follow up question. "How do you know?"

Adam lifted the gun and aimed through the sight at a tree in the distance. "Trust me. I know."

Flexing his chest, Colt pointed in Adam's direction. "Wait a minute. Who put you in charge?"

Wolf walked up confidently and placed a firm hand on Adam's shoulder. "I trust him."

A debate took off from there, with each member of the group voicing their concern. Ultimately, the Red team agreed to follow Adam, some more reluctantly than others.

Martinez's voice then boomed into the warehouse over a loudspeaker. "Begin."

Adam immediately crouched down and gestured his hand towards an opening in the forest. "This way."

Shaking his head, Colt grunted a response to Adam's suggestion and walked off in a different direction, without uttering a word.

They all watched him leave, but Hawk was the only one to do so with a smile. "I give him two minutes."

Heading out into the forest, Adam and the three girls crouched low in a half circle, just wide enough so they could all see each other as they moved through the trees. Leading the way up front, Adam knelt down and put his hand up to halt the girls behind him. He examined a footprint in the mud then signaled Tiger to head left. She moved slowly, but then suddenly pointed and shot at movement in the trees above.

The muffled gunshot barely let out a light whistle, but nothing fell from the branches overhead. She waited a second, examining the area with her gun still aimed at the ready. A dart then abruptly flew into the girl's neck, and a moment later her eyes fluttered shut.

Before Tiger's unconscious body even hit the ground, the remaining Red team members took cover behind the trees. Adam quickly scanned the forest floor for more footprints, but his concentration was broken as Falcon abruptly dropped to the ground in front of him. Reacting on instinct, Adam aimed and shot, hitting the girl before she had a chance return to fire. He then quickly looked up and found the members of Blue team leaping between the branches above him. "They're up in the trees! All of them!"

Wolf, Adam, and Hawk immediately lifted their pistols and

shot randomly into the trees. Blue team returned fire and a wave of darts crossed paths, heading high and low and in between. Toad and Hound soon fell from the treetops and landed firmly in the mud, but not before Hawk was hit and taken out of the battle.

In one smooth motion, Adam dropped the clip out of his M9 and reloaded with another. "Wolf, regroup. Follow me."

Adam and Wolf started running through the forest, quickly coming across Colt's unconscious body.

"Ignore him," said Adam while hopping over his unconscious squad mate. "Keep moving."

They eventually exited the forest into an open field, and Wolf instantly spotted Ox taking aim from beside them. "Lion, look out!"

She mechanically aimed and fired, hitting Ox center mass. The girl smiled at her perfect shot, until being startled by Travis grabbing her from behind. He quickly put his gun's silenced barrel to her neck and pulled the trigger. The weapon didn't make a sound. Not even a whisper.

Hoping to thank Wolf for the save, Adam turned back around from watching Ox fall and found Travis dropping Wolf's sleeping body to the grass. With lighting reflexes, both boys raised their guns and took aim at one another. Standing only a few feet away, they locked eyes and stared each other down, their faces completely emotionless and detached from any other thought but winning.

More curious than confused, the man in the suit leaned forward in his stance and squinted at the monitors across the room. "What are they doing?"

"I'm not sure," replied Martinez, also squinting at the screens.

With their fingers gently caressing the triggers, Adam and Travis continued to glare at one another for several seconds. They didn't speak a word or show any other sign, yet out of nowhere they both began kneeling slowly while swinging their weapons out to the side. With their arms extended, the boys continued their stare down, before abruptly dropping their guns at the same time and charging straight ahead.

Travis struck first, tackling Adam to the ground and immediately gaining the upper hand. Entwined around one another, the boys rolled through the field until colliding into a fist-sized rock. Adam took position on top of his opponent and delivered a hard punch to Travis's jaw, but the pinned boy didn't even respond to the blow and threw Adam straight off of him.

"This is not part of the exercise," barked Martinez, shaking his head. "I'm stopping them."

The Major moved to place his hand on the intercom in front of them, but the man in the suit reached out to stop him. "Are you kidding? This is finally getting interesting."

Locked in a grapple, Travis moved to trip his opponent, but Adam quickly spun around, swiping Travis's leg out from under him. As Travis hit the ground, Adam was already on top of him, driving his knee into his rival's throat.

"Not a dart, but it does the trick."

Travis began fighting against Adam's leg, futilely trying to force it off of him. Struggling to breathe, the boy started aimlessly reaching around until his hand came across the small rock they had bumped into earlier. He grabbed onto it hard and bashed the front of his attacker's knee. Adam screamed and jerked his knee back in pain, releasing Travis from the chokehold.

Gasping for air, Travis coughed several times while desperately crawling away. He soon spotted an M9 lying in the grass and slithered towards it as Adam caught sight of where he was headed and launched himself to intercept.

Reaching out, Travis grabbed the gun, rolled over to his back, and fired just as Adam dove straight out for him. The dart stuck Adam in the chest as he flew through the air, and he was out cold before hitting the ground.

With the show finally over, the entertained man smiled at Martinez while nodding his head. "Interesting. I think I'll meet the boy now."

"Fox?" asked the Major as the man started moving past him.

"No." The man shook his head while continuing towards the door. "The other one."

"But sir, Fox was the winner," said Martinez, believing he was correcting a mistake.

The man replied without ever stopping or turning around from his departure. "That may be, but who grabbed the gun?"

# 10

The following day, the children were having lunch in the cafeteria when Martinez called for Adam to finish his meal and follow him. Something like that had never happened before, so the rest of the group watched anxiously as the boy returned his tray and went with the Major across the room.

They approached a table and found Christine, Jason, and a third man dressed in a suit, calmly waiting for them.

Martinez motioned for Adam to sit down. "Have a seat, Lion."

He did cautiously, hesitantly, and somewhat confused. "What's going on?"

Martinez sat down at the table as well. "Jason, Christine, and I have been impressed with your progress. You showed excellent leadership skills in the exercise yesterday."

Christine gently placed her hands on top of Adam's. It was the most affection he'd received from another human being since leaving St. Maria's.

"All the analysts," she said, "Jason and myself included, have chosen you to be squad leader. It's a big responsibility. The lives of nine people are in your hands now. If you want the job, of course."

Jason then gestured towards the man in the suit. "This is our supervisor, Mr. Hopkins. He works with our funding and pretty much manages everything that goes on here."

The man put on a grin much wider than anyone would naturally display and extended an open hand towards Adam. "Hello, Lion. Nice to meet you."

Adam looked at the man sideways for a moment before

shaking his head, making a point that he wasn't going to accept the handshake. "Don't do that."

"Do what?" asked Hopkins, curious at the boy's refusal.

"Act like you care about me. I can tell you don't. In fact, you probably don't care about any of us. All you care about are your cool little toys being built behind these walls, right? Which is fine. I have warm food and a bed to sleep in because of you. But don't ever pretend to be my friend, because you're not."

The man's face slowly rose into an amused smirk, a far more conceited yet genuine expression than the one he had shown before. "You're right, Jason. The boy has spunk."

Hopkins then leaned forward across the table, bringing his face close enough to whisper, yet his voice grew even louder than before. "Now listen here, kid. As impressed as I was watching you yesterday, you're right. I *don't* care about you. You're a study. An experiment. The 'cool toys' I have behind these walls will change the world. Something you will never accomplish."

"Ha. Like what?" asked Adam sarcastically. "A big bomb. Ooh, scary."

The smirk returned as the man leaned back in his seat, rubbing his chin in thought. "You know what? Come on. I have something to show you."

Hopkins stood first and Adam followed, as did Martinez, nervously trying to stop them from leaving. "I don't think this is such a good idea."

Hopkins placed a firm hand on Martinez's shoulder, a move of authority masked as a reassuring gesture. "Don't worry. The boy has a right to understand his place in all this. He'll be fine. Now go brief the children on their new squad leader. Jason and Christine, get back to work. Let's take a walk, son."

Hopkins began to exit the cafeteria, with Adam trailing behind him. On their way, Adam briefly caught a glimpse of the children's table and saw them all curiously watching him leave.

Adam followed Hopkins through The Armory and down several halls he had never been in before. Like most of the place, they looked like generic office building corridors, with bright florescent lights and bland grey wallpaper.

Eventually they came to a strange elevator that had no numbers on the many buttons inside, yet Hopkins pressed one without even thinking about it. "So what's your name, kid?" The doors of the elevator closed and Adam remained standing at attention. "Lion."

Hopkins rolled his eyes. "Yeah, I never was a fan of talking in code. So why don't you tell me your real name?"

"I forgot," stated Adam, still at attention.

Hopkins relaxed his stance and leaned against the elevator wall. "Oh, don't give me that. Just because you don't like me doesn't mean we can't have a normal conversation."

Adam's stiffened back slouched ever so slightly as he lowered his head. "... Adam."

"Hmmm. Adam. How ironic," noted Hopkins with a veiled smirk.

Adam looked up, curious by his comment. "Why is that—"

He was cut off as the elevator opened and Hopkins exited before the doors had fully moved out of the way. "Here we are."

They both stepped out into another long hallway similar to the last, and Hopkins led the boy forward with a gentle hand on his back. "Now, Adam, people like to talk about the economy's collapse as a national crisis, but that's not necessarily true. It's a *global* one. This whole planet is constantly on the brink of war. Every country in the world is turning inward; building their armies, strengthening their people, so that when this political pressure cooker pops, they will be prepared for the conflict that comes with it. Our nation is no different. In order to ensure a quick victory we need an advantage that our enemies do not have. A force, whether it be a weapon or something else, that will overwhelm them quickly before the conflict escalates."

As they continued to move ahead, Hopkins placed a proud hand on his chest. "That's where I come in. I'm in charge of creating that advantage—and this facility is where it will be discovered. For instance, with over four hundred thousand children desperate for a future, the orphans we have stuck in the federal system are a treasure trove of potential soldiers just waiting to be conscripted. You and your team are part of a study to turn those orphans into a cohesive and efficient fighting force."

"Sounds illegal," Adam reasonably noted.

Hopkins appeared unconcerned with the distinction. "We're the government, Adam. We don't let trivial obstacles like laws and ethics get in our way."

He then stopped in the middle of the hall and turned to face the boy that had been walking alongside him. "Take another project we've been working on, for example. I have several scientists designing a mutagenic serum that will fundamentally alter a subject's DNA, to the point of superhuman abilities."

Adam's face scrunched, a clear sign of his skepticism. "That's impossible."

Opening his shoulder, Hopkins gestured to a steel door behind him. "Then why don't you tell that to our friend Stryker?"

The door had no signs or fixtures. Not even a doorknob. The only marker that it was even there was a small keypad on the wall next to it, which Hopkins leaned into and began entering a long sequence of numbers. "In his prime, Robert Stryker was the best soldier this country had ever seen. Loyal, disciplined, and a fighter with the instinctual drive to win at all costs. He was also the first test subject to receive the super-soldier serum."

The door quickly slid open, revealing nothing but darkness behind it. Hopkins stood up straight and motioned for Adam to enter. "Now he's … well … I'll let you see for yourself."

Both cautious and curious at the same time, Adam took several slow steps into the dark room before turning back around. "There's nothing here."

The boy was suddenly slammed from behind, his body thrown against a wall in the darkness. The room's lights sporadically flickered on to reveal a hideous green monster, standing nearly ten feet high and wrapped in chains around its arms and neck. A random assortment of horns poked through the creature's gruesomely scarred face, and its scaly skin, bulging around its thick muscles and chest, shimmered in the dim light.

*Stryker.* It was the name Hopkins had called the monstrosity. He swiped his clawed hand out at Adam, but the boy's training instantly took over, regardless of the bizarre foe standing before him. He rolled out of the claw's way and kicked back up to his feet, to run at Stryker's talon-covered foot. The monster lifted up its leg and stomped down, another attack that Adam evaded. As a follow-up, Stryker brutishly swung his other arm around and grabbed Adam's entire body in his claws. Although he held his own longer than expected, Adam was now trapped in the monster's grasp and shrieked in pain as Stryker squeezed.

Hopkins casually walked through the doorway, unsympathetic to the boy's tortured screams. "Big fella, isn't he? Ok. I think that's enough."

A jolt of electricity suddenly ran up the monster's chains and the beast let out a howl of agony. He released his hold on Adam and the boy dropped to the floor, before quickly scurrying back to the hallway. Hopkins then nonchalantly backed up himself and the steel door slammed shut, as Stryker continued to wail devilishly on the other side.

Trying to catch his breath, Adam leaned up against the wall to recover, and Hopkins took advantage of the boy's weakened state by strutting towards him. "You see, Adam? That's why you don't matter. Because against that, you and your friends are nothing."

As Adam still struggled to control his wild gasps for air, his focus was diverted to a woman approaching them from down the hall. "What are you doing outside this door, Jack?"

Hopkins nodded at the woman with a sarcastic smile. "Good to see you too, Vanessa."

She had long, straight black hair and a fit body, clearly in far better shape than the aged wrinkles on her face suggested.

Vanessa marched towards them and stopped with perfect posture. "Answer the question."

Hopkins preserved the same arrogant smirk as he gestured towards Adam beside him.

"I was just giving Lion here the pleasure of meeting your husband."

Vanessa glanced over at Adam just long enough to become shocked by what she heard. "You put this kid in there with him? What's wrong with you?"

"He actually lasted far longer than I anticipated," said Hopkins while nodding his head, impressed.

Vanessa stepped forward, merely inches from Hopkins's face. "Robert's not your little pet. Don't treat him like one."

Hopkins stared back at her, letting his smile gradually fade away. "I think you're forgetting who is in charge here, Vanessa."

Adam finally found the energy to press up off the wall and interrupt them, asking the question he'd wanted to voice earlier. "*That* was your husband?"

"That IS my husband," corrected Vanessa. "And one day we will find a cure for what this man has done to him."

Hopkins gently placed a caring hand on the woman's shoulder. "I promised you I would make it right again, and I will."

"You better, Hopkins." She brushed off his hand while starting to move past him. "And don't touch me."

As Vanessa continued on down the hall, Adam watched her perfect figure sway back and forth with every step. "You're not looking for a cure, are you?"

Hopkins answered while also staring at Vanessa walking away from them.

"Stryker's a soldier. Just like his wife. As far as I'm concerned, the only cure for that is death."

"You're an asshole, you know that," Adam remarked, looking up at him.

Hopkins held in a single chuckle and turned to lead the boy back the way they came. "I know, Adam. I know."

# 11

Eight months had passed since the children first woke up in The Armory, but to them, it felt more like years. Every day they continued with the same rigorous routine of training. It was composed of lessons in the classrooms, combat scenarios in the warehouse, target practice on the range, workouts in the weight room, and brutal sparring sessions in the gym. If Martinez believed something could improve their skills as soldiers, then the children had no choice but to comply.

And they did.

As squad leader, Adam quickly gained the respect of the others and successfully organized them into a single, cohesive unit. But against Martinez's orders, he had begun to form a friendship with Travis Sky. The boy codenamed Fox.

Although they worked in multiple rooms throughout The Armory, the squad typically did their hand-to-hand combat training in a tightly-enclosed gymnasium with mats covering the floor. In order to mix things up, Martinez had the ten children rotating partners for every session.

Adam understood his logic. It made sense not to get accustomed to fighting one person. But he always looked forward to the days when he was paired with Travis. It was the only time he actually felt like he was being challenged.

With the rest of the squad already engaged in close-quarters combat, Adam and Travis took their time getting ready in the far corner of the room. As Adam finished putting on his gear, Travis started to tease him, dangling a blindfold in front of his face. "What do you say we make this interesting?"

Adam briefly looked up from tying his shoe to wave Travis off. "We're supposed to be practicing. Not sparring. Put it away."

"Martinez doesn't care," said Travis while still holding up the blindfold. "Come on."

Adam finished tying his shoe and stood up, annoyed. "You're going to get us in trouble again. This is just a training session."

Travis put up his hands in a soft fighting stance and began jokingly throwing punches. "What? Are you scared I might kick your ass like that time I burned you on the track?"

"I got a cramp," said Adam, rolling his eyes. "You didn't burn me."

"Excuses, excuses. It's always excuses with you."

Clenching his teeth in frustration, Adam finally gave in and held out his hand. "Fine. Give it to me."

Travis smiled as he threw Adam the blindfold. "That-a-boy."

The two of them moved over onto the mat and stood across from one another, while wrapping their blindfolds over their eyes. They then both took strong fighting stances and began slowly creeping in a circle.

The standoff lasted several seconds, neither boy drawing up the courage to strike, until Adam felt the urge to mock his opponent. "What's wrong, Fox? You always make the first move."

Rather than being provoked though, Travis just laughed off the insult. "It's a little bit harder when I can't see."

"Now who has the excuses?" Adam taunted again.

Travis then suddenly kicked forward. Sensing the attack, Adam ducked out of the way and threw a follow-up punch towards his opponent's midsection. Travis caught his fist before it struck and pushed Adam off, allowing them both to resume their stances.

Once again resuming their battle, both boys carefully tested each other's moves and counters, reacting with a combination of instinct and training. Like an orchestrated dance, the fight progressed slowly at first, until the young warriors felt comfortable enough to speed up their attacks. It wasn't long before punches and kicks were being thrown from every angle, at lightning speeds, far faster than their training session warranted.

The skirmish quickly grabbed the attention of everyone in the room. The other children pretended to keep practicing, but their eyes were really focused on the two best fighters amongst them, going at it in the corner. They expected Martinez to step in and stop the fight, but the Major simply stood in the doorway, spectating as well.

Travis swung for a hook and missed, prompting Adam to resume his taunts. "Too slow, Foxy."

"Stop calling me that!"

Travis swept his leg around and tripped Adam to the floor. With his back against the mat, Adam heard Travis's foot thrusting down on top of him and barely managed to bring his hands up to catch in it. He then pushed Travis back and kicked himself up onto his feet.

Setting themselves up for a finishing blow, the two fighters threw punches at the exact same time. Realizing what was about to happen first, Travis opened up his hand and grabbed onto Adam's arm instead. He then twisted Adam's elbow back around his head, locking the boy into submission. "Ahhh. You smell that? Victory."

"No," said Adam, gritting his teeth through the pain. "You just need to shower."

"Is there ever a time you're not joking, Lion?"

Adam writhed in place, trying to loosen Travis's hold. "The only joke here is how easily I'm going to beat you right now."

"Be my guest. I'll break your arm before you—"

Adam abruptly threw his other elbow back, nailing his captor in the chin. He then quickly turned around and hooked Travis with his now-free arm. The hard blow knocked Travis to the floor and he rolled over exhausted, letting himself sink into the mat while taking off his blindfold. "Lucky punch."

Smiling, Adam pulled his own blindfold down around his neck and extended his hand to lift Travis up off the ground.

As the two boys dusted themselves off following the bout, Martinez casually walked over to the mat while clapping slowly. "Impressive. But you better watch out for that elbow, Fox. It's going to get you killed one of these days."

He then turned to look out over the other children in the room. "All right, everyone. Take five."

They all dispersed to the water cooler and bathroom, while Travis and Adam walked over to sit down together on a bench by the corner. Still aching from the blow, Travis couldn't stop rubbing his chin, while Adam closed his eyes and rested his head against the wall. "You know, Travis, you're the closest thing I've ever had to a real friend."

"That's pretty sad," said Travis with his jaw stretched open.

Adam responded with his eyes still closed. "Story of my life."

Travis turned and placed a hand on his friend's shoulder. "Well, just so you know, when we step onto a real battlefield there's no one else I would rather have leading this team."

Adam opened his eyes with an appreciative smile. "Thanks, man."

"No, Adam. Thank you."

# 12

In the weeks that passed, the children continued their workouts and training during the day. But during the night, the images of a dying father that had once plagued Adam's mind were now replaced with the monster Stryker had become. He would lie in bed at night, staring up at the barracks' ceiling and imaging what it must've been like to possess such strength. *To feel as if every human walking around you was nothing compared to your power.* And the thought excited him to his core.

Eventually, Adam couldn't take the wondering anymore. He needed to learn more about Stryker and his story. He craved to know who he was and where he came from. But Adam wasn't naïve. He knew he had to talk to someone he could trust, and only two people came to mind.

Surprisingly, Jason and Christine had been like a brother and sister to Adam ever since he arrived at The Armory. They'd looked out for him when he never expected them to, especially when Martinez was at his worst. Adam trusted them to tell him the truth about the monster that attacked him—assuming they even knew it to begin with.

After sneaking away from a lifting session, Adam went to their shared office and poked his head inside from the hall. "Hey."

The room was small, practically a closet, and consisted of two desks arranged in a V formation, with Jason and Christine each seated behind one, and an empty chair in between them.

Christine looked up after Adam made himself known, but Jason was the one to greet him, with his eyes still focused on his paperwork. "Shouldn't you be in the weight room?"

"I need to ask you guys something," said Adam, ignoring the analyst's question.

"What is it?" asked Christine, both curious and concerned at the same time.

"What can you tell me about Robert Stryker and the super-soldier project?"

Jason froze for a moment before slowly looking up from his work. "Martinez was right. Hopkins should have never told you about what goes on here. The less you know about The Armory the better."

Christine shrugged her shoulders with a regretful grimace. "Sorry, Lion. I wish we could help."

Undeterred by their reluctance, Adam moved further into the doorway, placing both hands on the frame. "You don't understand. I need to know."

Christine stood from her desk and walked around to place a hand on Adam's shoulder. "Come on, Jason. Tell him what you know. What's the worst that could happen?"

"I'm gonna regret this," Jason sighed to himself. "Fine. Shut the door and take a seat."

Christine flashed Adam a wink and then left the room as he entered it. Adam closed the door behind him and sat down in the lone chair between the desks.

"Now, listen," started Jason, clasping his hands in front of him. "What I'm about to tell you is highly classified information. Even I'm not supposed to know it; but it's impossible to keep a secret in this place. Everyone finds out everything eventually. Still, what we're about to discuss stays in this room and you didn't hear it from me."

Adam sat up straight with his back against the seat. "Understood."

Jason took a deep, lasting breath before continuing on. "Robert Stryker was part of a highly skilled special ops unit where he met his wife, Vanessa. Second in command behind Stryker was someone you know all too well: Christopher Martinez."

"Are you serious?" asked Adam, completely surprised.

Jason nodded with a smirk. "Yup. Martinez had a wife in the unit, too. People were always cracking jokes about them double-dating on missions. But there was also a fifth member of the team. A man named Andrew Tyran."

Adam leaned forward as the story started to grab his interest. "What happened?"

"As a unit, the five of them were a force of nature. No mission seemed too impossible or too dangerous for them to complete. Over time though, Tyran became obsessed with Martinez's wife. He grew jealous and couldn't stand to see them together. So one day, Tyran flipped. He defected and began working for a group called Molotok."

"Molotok?"asked Adam, unfamiliar with the word.

"It's Russian. Means 'The Hammer'. They're an underground movement within the Russian Federation's military. Deeply secretive, deeply fanatical, and hell bent on destroying the West. They hold our government responsible for the world's economic meltdown, and when Hopkins talks about an enemy, that's usually who he's referring to."

Jason paused for Adam to ask a question, but continued on when he didn't. "Stryker's unit was planning a large operation to cut off their supply line in the Middle East, but Molotok was waiting for them and sprung a trap. The unit managed to escape unharmed, but by the time they realized Tyran had betrayed them, it was too late. He took Martinez's wife hostage and threatened to flee to Russia. When she fought back, he killed her right in front of them. Watching his wife die did something to Martinez. He snapped and went after Tyran, stealing the man's knife and slicing up his face. He probably would've killed him, too, if Stryker hadn't stepped in and stopped him."

"So how did Stryker get here?" asked Adam, eager to know more.

"I'm getting there. This all happened about two years ago. I have no idea where they took Tyran, but rumor is they have him locked up in a dungeon prison somewhere and threw away the key."

Adam's eyebrows rose, as he momentarily put himself in Tyran's shoes. "He must be pissed."

"I'm sure he is," agreed Jason, nodding his head. "But he succeeded in destroying the unit. None of them wanted to be in the field again. So they were assigned here, instead. As you know, Martinez became your instructor, while Stryker and his wife donated their bodies to the super-soldier project.

"But there was a problem during Stryker's operation. The procedure failed and he became ... well ... whatever he is now. The scientists went back to the formula after that, trying to figure out what went wrong. As for Vanessa, her version of the serum was put on hold and she's been waiting for her turn ever since."

Adam sat in silence for a moment, allowing the full craziness of Stryker's tale to sink in. Jason didn't say a word. He simply watched the boy come to grips with everything he'd heard.

After about a minute, Adam thanked Jason for his help and left the office, passing Christine where she was waiting in the hall just outside the door. He walked straight past her on his way back to the weight room, without saying goodbye.

It wasn't that he intentionally ignored her. He just had thoughts of Stryker weighing heavy on his mind.

# 13

Ten months into their training, Martinez was starting to believe the children were almost ready for combat. They were no longer being separated into groups during their scenarios, but training as a complete squad against actual soldiers armed with electric shock ammunition. Not every simulation was a success, but through their failures they all learned to work as a single cohesive unit, with each member as an extension of the whole.

The children understood each other's strengths and weakness, and could predict each other's movements and attacks. It wasn't long before Martinez was struggling to come up with further unique missions and objectives for them to accomplish, each exercise more dangerous than the last.

In the continuously-shifting warehouse environment, the Major established a brutal urban warfare setting, inspired by the ruins of Eastern Europe. On the outskirts of what appeared to be a devastated community littered with bombed-out buildings and rubble-filled streets, Martinez lined up the squad and stood before them to deliver his briefing. "This is enemy-controlled territory. Intelligence suggests that the civilian population has been evacuated, so assume all encounters to be hostile. Your mission is the capture of important enemy documents, located somewhere in the city."

After the formal briefing as commander, Martinez assumed the role of instructor and began pacing up and down the line of children. "There is to be no radio communication during the mission. I want you focus on using the hand signals we practiced last week. All combat tactics and strategies we've gone over thus far should be at your disposal. You have two hours to accomplish your objective. If you suffer a casualty, you will run wind sprints an hour straight for every man down. If you fail the mission, then don't plan on eating tomorrow, because you'll be running wind sprints the entire day. Good luck."

Martinez walked through the line, exiting through a door in the corner of the warehouse.

Once he was gone, Adam unfolded a map from his pocket and moved quickly to organize his squad. "There are at least a hundred buildings here. We can't search them all in time if we stick together, so we'll have to split up. Fox, take Tiger, Toad, Hawk, and Hound. Head through the back alley over there and come around from the north side. I'll take the rest of the squad and we'll head in from the south. Meet at this building in the center of the city—and be extra cautious. Martinez is really gunning for us after we completed the last one without breaking a sweat."

Adam signaled to Fox and the two teams, armed with a wide assortment of rifles modified for the exercise, broke off to head in opposite directions. Carefully traversing the cityscape, Adam's group cut through an alley branching off from a nearby street. He then stopped and signaled back to Falcon, who began scaling the building's fire escape, taking to a roof for sniper cover.

Turning his attention to Colt and Ox, Adam ordered them both into position on either side of him and started heading down the street, with Wolf watching the rear.

For nearly an hour, the group slowly swept the neighborhood in perfect formation. They went building to building, searching for the enemy base, all the while covering every angle for a possible ambush.

Eventually, Adam came to a run-down multi-family house and approached the front door, much like any other. As he reached for the doorknob, the body of an electrified enemy soldier suddenly hit the ground beside him. Adam looked up to the roof across the street and saw Falcon signaling rapidly to him. It was a warning of increased enemy activity around the area.

Adam then directed his attention to Colt and Ox, ordering them to go around back while he and Wolf headed through the front.

Once inside the building, the pair of armed teenagers slowly made their way down the hall with their M4 assault rifles aimed at the ready. Paint chips and damp furniture covered the warped and twisted wooden floor. The walls, every one looking about ready to collapse, opened up around a staircase, which served as the house's main focal point.

Adam cautiously signaled Wolf to head up to the second floor, but she broke operational silence as movement from overhead abruptly caught her eye.

"Fire from above!"

Without even looking to see what she'd spotted, Adam dove to the ground for cover, as several loud gunshots peppered the wall around him. Dropping to the floor as well, Wolf safely crawled into another room, but Adam wasn't so lucky, pinned down by a shooter at the top of the stairs. He took immediate shelter behind an overturned dresser in the middle of the hallway. The enemy continued to fire at the old wooden piece of furniture, tearing it apart piece by piece with every blast.

Trapped, Adam looked around for a way to get free, as did Wolf from the safety of her room above. She soon realized, though, that the house didn't have a back entrance. "Lion, there's no way for Colt and Ox to get through here."

Adam sat up straight with his back planted firmly against the disintegrating dresser. "They won't make it in time anyway."

"I have an idea," said Wolf optimistically. "If you give me a little cover fire, I think I have a shot."

Adam shook his head, rejecting the plan. "No. You don't. He's kneeling by the banister."

But Wolf persisted. "I can make the shot. Give me a chance."

Rather than respond, Adam ignored her completely, taking matters into his own hands. In one swift motion, he lifted what was left of the dresser off the ground, flipping it over onto its side, with himself still behind it. Distracted by the sudden maneuver, the enemy's fire halted for a split second, just long enough for Adam to fire a single shot and take him out.

Once the area was clear, Adam stood up and dusted himself off as Wolf left her room to confront him. "What the hell was that?"

Adam opened his mouth to answer, but was interrupted by Ox entering the building with the enemy documents in hand. Wolf was eager to continue their conversation, but Adam was already headed back outside. Once they were together, the rest of the group made their way back to the rendezvous point and simulated an exfiltration for another successful mission.

Later in the day, Wolf waited until just before lights out in the barracks before confronting Adam again. "Are we going to talk about what happened out there today?"

"Why? What happened?" asked Adam, walking past her towards his bed.

"I could've made that shot," said Wolf, following behind him. "Just a little distraction and I would've had him."

Uninterested in the discussion, Adam shrugged his shoulders while unfolding the sheets on his bed. "It doesn't matter. We got out of it."

Annoyed by his response, Wolf moved over to stand beside him and make her opinion known. "That's not the point. You don't trust me. You've never trusted me. I've saved your ass so many times, and you still don't think I can pull through."

Still refusing to look at her, Adam waved his hand and turned to walk away. "I'm not having this discussion with you."

Wolf reached out and grabbed his arm, stopping him from leaving. "No, Adam. Look at me. I've seen you trust the others. But why not me? You think you're better than me? Just because you're squad leader doesn't mean—"

Adam suddenly pulled his arm away from her grasp, cutting her off. "You want to know why, Sarah? You honestly what to know why I can't trust you with my life?"

"Yes," she said, practically begging for an answer.

"Do you have feelings for me?"

"*What?*" asked Wolf, caught off guard by the question. "Why should it matter if—"

"Just answer it."

Wolf swallowed deeply, hiding her embarrassment before responding. "Yeah. I like you. So what?"

Adam looked her straight in the eyes, his face and words as stern as could be. "Well, you heard what Martinez said. We're not friends. We can't be. One day, the time will come when you will have to decide between me and the success of our mission. The choice should be easy."

Wolf began to protest. "But—"

Adam put his hand up, stopping her argument before it even began. "No buts. As long as you care about me as more than your squad leader, then your judgment will be off."

Wolf's face sank in betrayed disappointment. "Adam ..."

Her voice trailed off, hoping the boy would somehow change his mind on his own, but while his face softened from its rigid defiance, he could only regretfully shake his head in response. "I'm sorry, but those feelings are pointless, and you need to get over them. Until then, I'd rather rely on myself."

Adam turned and walked away, leaving the girl standing alone in the middle of the barracks.

# 14

Two long years later, and Hopkins had grown mixed feelings about the overall progress of his work. While many programs at his facility had moved along nicely, some had become stalled in perpetual limbo. The ultimate goal of his mission had remained total dominance of the battlefield, but military research and development was a never-ending struggle. For every break-through he made, Hopkins feared his enemy was already five steps ahead.

He spent much of those years in his office, an elegantly spacious room with a hardwood interior, located in an isolated corner of the facility. Hopkins very rarely held meetings or conferences there. The space was his only private retreat, where he could conduct his work in solitude. But after hearing that Dr. Groves, the lead scientist on the super-soldier project, wanted to speak with him, Hopkins could think of no better place to entertain the doctor's request.

While looking over a list of the facility's inventory, the phone on Hopkins's desk lit up, indicating the doctor had arrived. Hopkins buzzed him in and a short, unimposing man in a white lab coat entered the room.

Hopkins looked up from his paperwork, but never stood from behind his desk as he gestured to the chair in front of it. "Good afternoon, Dr. Groves. Please. Have a seat."

Brushing a few greasy strands of hair across his balding head, Groves walked over to the chair and sat down with a wide smile on his face. "Thank you for making time for me, Mr. Hopkins."

"I made time for my serum," said Hopkins while clasping

his hands on the desk. "Now do you have any good news, or just the same old disappointments?"

Groves's eyes grew wide with excitement and optimism. "We're making progress with the formula. However, we need live test subjects."

Hopkins shook his head in a grimace. "I gave you those embryos, didn't I? Finding ones within your parameters was not an easy task."

Groves brought his hands together on his lap, pressing his ten fingers into one another. "Yes. And I appreciate that. We learned a lot from them. But a human embryo can only go so far in research. We need full grown specimens."

Bored and frustrated with the conversation, Hopkins's attention went back to the inventory on his desk. "The answer is still no. The last thing I need is another Robert Stryker walking around."

Frustrated as well, Groves inched forward to the edge of his seat. "Sir, our work has come a long way since then. Our methods have changed and a genetic transformation on that scale is highly unlikely."

"Highly unlikely?" asked Groves, his eyes briefly looking up from his paperwork before returning to it. "That doesn't fill me with confidence."

"Well, a scientist never deals in absolutes. You have to understand, everything we're doing here is theoretical. My team and I are literally creating a new scientific field as we work."

Dropping the paper he held in his hand, Hopkins stood from his seat and leaned forward over his desk. "I'm serious, doctor. I don't want an army of monsters. Now tell me: can you deliver me the super human you promised, or not?"

Groves awkwardly smiled, reluctant to give the man the answer he was looking for. "We aren't sure. Without a proper trial and error process, it's impossible to know what the outcome will be. I need to run some more tests. Perhaps if we pick up some homeless individuals off the street? People no one will miss?"

Tilting his head to the side in annoyance, Hopkins began walking around to the front of his desk. "Are you kidding me?

What if it works? Did you think of that? A bum walking around with that kind of power?"

As Hopkins reached him, Dr. Groves stood and clumsily adjusted his wrinkled lab coat. "Well then, what do you want me to do?"

Hopkins put his hands on the scientist's shoulders and leaned in close enough to smell his body odor. "Do what you do best, doctor. Figure it out. I have faith you'll find a way."

# 15

Now sixteen years of age, Adam remained both squad leader and the youngest of the group. They were still being studied and watched, their every move analyzed for the purposes of the program, but the teenagers were no longer trainees. They were now veteran fighters with actual field experience under their belt.

The missions they'd been assigned had all been of minimal risk on American soil. Raids and hostage situations, caused by pockets of rebellion against the government. The group as a whole had yet to be deployed on an actual foreign battlefield.

That was about to change.

While the rest of the squad chatted amongst themselves, seated in the briefing room, Adam quietly waited in a corner. He was meditating, gathering his thoughts in the calm before the storm.

He stood suddenly, tall and proud, as Martinez entered the room with a stack of folders tucked under his arm. "Officer on deck!"

In unison, the entire unit silenced themselves and shot up at attention. Martinez stood by the door for a moment to admire their discipline, before motioning them to sit back down. "At ease."

The group returned to their seats and Martinez walked forward to the center of the room. "I know you're all feeling a little anxious and excited. Maybe even nervous. Good. You should be. You've been training for two years to go abroad. That's a long time. But you've already had many flawless missions here at home. You're ready for this. I wouldn't have signed off on it otherwise. Just remember, you're more than soldiers. So act like it."

After his speech, Martinez walked around the room to hand out the folders to his troops. "You'll be headed to Afghanistan for your first international mission. It's an important one, too. A base there belongs to an underground organization our intelligence community believes to be actively plotting against the U.S. The base itself is an old decommissioned Soviet facility from last century's Cold War. It's located in the middle of nowhere, a thousand feet under the desert. However, the only entrance is three miles away in a nearby village. A tramline provides transportation between the two."

Once all the folders had been handed out, they sat on desks untouched as Martinez returned to the center of the room and continued to speak. "Because of the base's isolation, it's quite difficult to infiltrate. Any movement of ground forces stationed in the area and the place will lock down before our troops get close to the door. That's where you come in. This unit has shown an impressive ability to get behind enemy lines undetected, which is exactly what you need to do if this mission is to become a success. Now please, open your intel files."

The squad began flipping through the folders as Martinez continued his briefing. "Our objective is to gather intelligence on the enemy's chain of command. Our source says there are blueprints within the base that lay out the enemy's leadership structure. Read these folders carefully. They contain all your mission parameters. You deploy in one hour. Good luck and dismissed."

Knowing not to ask any more questions, the squad quietly stood and began filing from the briefing room with their folders in hand. Adam was the last one to exit, but stopped just short of the door and turned back to Martinez. "It's them, isn't it?"

"It's who?" asked the Major, not appearing at all confused by the question.

"The base," clarified Adam. "It belongs to them, doesn't it?"

Martinez sternly stared through the boy rather than at him, and held the glare a moment before answering. "I don't know what you're talking about, soldier, but you know better than to ask."

Adam nodded once, confirming that he had received the unspoken message. "Sorry, sir."

He turned and walked through door, sensing Martinez's eyes piercing him from behind.

Sand sprang up and spun wildly through the air as two vans draped in camouflage rode fast across the cracked desert earth. Inside the speeding vehicles, Adam and his squad approached a small isolated village of tents and cinderblock structures in the distance.

After swerving around the perimeter of the dilapidated community, the vans abruptly cut through the center of the township and stopped behind what appeared to be an inconspicuous building held together by mud and stones. The doors to the vans shot open and all ten of the troops, drivers included, seamlessly flowed around the building for cover. They all held their M16 assault rifles firm against their shoulders, searching the apparently empty village for any signs of movement.

Only Ox had his attention elsewhere, focused on disabling a rather out-of-place security panel attached to the side of the structure. A moment later, the building's steel door popped open, clearing the way for Hawk and Falcon to lob two smoke grenades inside.

As a dense cloud quickly filled the room, Adam signaled Tiger and Colt to storm in next. They moved swiftly through the smoke, silently coming up on the two guards and knocking them out before they even realized what was going on. The smoke cleared a moment later and the rest of the squad poured into the small concrete room. Its contents consisted of a security desk and a small door leading down to a stairwell.

Adam motioned for Toad to monitor the surveillance system, as several guards below began to make their way upstairs. Just before they reached the door, Toad signaled Fox and Wolf to kick the door open. The two opened fire, mowing the surprised guards down until none of them remained standing. Toad then scanned the other monitors for any remaining resistance.

"All clear."

Adam raised his arm, calling his team together to regroup. "We're going in. Tiger and Toad are to stay behind and hold the entrance down there. Don't let anyone through. The longer we can keep an alarm from going off the better. Everyone else, follow me."

Adam led the rest of the team down the stairwell and into a tram station, where a small tram sat waiting for them. It rested on a single track which led away into a tight tunnel, traversing about ten feet of light before plunging into darkness.

Once inside the tram, Hound took the controls, while the others grabbed onto the railings positioned around the cab's perimeter. As the tram lurched forward, the squad mechanically removed balaclava masks from their packs and pulled them over their faces.

They then began a final check of their gear as Adam delivered his last-minute orders. "We'll split up into two teams. Wolf, Fox, Hound, and I will make up Red team, while Falcon, Colt, Hawk, and Ox will be Blue. Remember, the base is going to be filled with soldiers, so be extra careful. Radio in when the blueprint is found. Let's go, boys and girls. Bring it home."

The tram slowed down before coming to a complete stop in a station similar to the one it had just departed. The only difference was that this one was heavily populated with men, all standing in front of two large metal doors against the station's far wall.

The tram doors shot open and both teams fluently exited, firing at will. Not expecting a barrage of gunfire, the men in front of the closed base doors were all dead within seconds.

Before the last guard even hit the floor, Adam had signaled Ox to arm the entrances with explosives. He worked fast, rigging the device and taking cover as his teammates got into position. Not a second later, Ox pulled the trigger and set off a large explosion that seared a hole straight through the impressive barricade in the station wall. The group then plunged through the opening, once again opening fire on anything standing in their path.

Together, both teams moved as deep as they could go into the base until the hallway split in two. Adam signaled Blue team to the left, and as Colt started to leave with his group, Adam reached out and grabbed his arm. "Remember, radio when you find it. I don't want us to be here one second longer than we have to."

"I have it covered," Colt replied, annoyed, ripping his arm away from Adam's grip. He then left at a trot, following his team down the hall.

Adam waited for him to turn a corner before leading his own group in the other direction through the bunker-like structure. Systematically checking every door and room they came across, Adam and the others scoured the place floor to ceiling and found nothing. Not even the slightest hint of resistance. Almost as if the entire base had been deserted beyond the opening hallway.

At the close of their search, Red team came to a dead end and Hound nervously lowered his gun. "This isn't right."

"Yeah," agreed Wolf, hopelessly searching the blocked corridor for a clue. "I got a bad feeling about this."

Fox opened his mouth to speak but was interrupted by sporadic static-chopped words from his radio. "… help … under fire … ambush …"

It was Colt's voice, drowned out by gunfire in the background.

"Back the way we came!" yelled Adam without the slightest bit of hesitation. "Hurry!"

In a dead sprint, Red team backtracked through the halls and down into the opposite side of the base. The tight hallway eventually opened up into a large, two-story mess hall with a balcony overlooking the room from the opposite side of the entrance. Standing against the balcony's railing was a squad of commandos covered head to toe in cybernetic body armor, far different from the cheap fatigues worn by the previous guards. They were also equipped with advanced sub-machine guns that continuously fired round after round down into the mess hall, without needing to be reloaded.

In the center of the room, Adam spotted a flipped-over

table, with Colt and Hawk taking cover behind it from the bombardment of gunfire. He also noticed Ox and Falcon's bodies lying on the floor, riddled with bullet holes and lying motionless in a pool of blood. Pushing thoughts of his fallen comrades aside, Adam recklessly dove through the gunfire to join his teammates still alive behind the table. The rest of Red team then turned over other tables as well and began to return fire at the commandos.

"What happened?" demanded Adam.

"It was an ambush," Colt replied. "They were waiting for us. As soon as we walked into the room, they gunned us down. Falcon and Ox had no chance. We just got lucky."

Hound peeked around the corner and noticed a shadow creeping up behind Hawk on the other side of the room. "Hawk, watch out behind—"

A bullet tore through the side of Hound's head, cutting off his sentence and splashing brain matter against the table. A wave of shock passing through her, Wolf began pulling his body back, as Hawk screamed out to him from across the room. "Hound!"

Adam turned to her and spotted a commando pointing a handgun to the back of her head. "No!"

It was too late. The commando pulled the trigger and taunted them in a Russian accent as Hawk's body dropped to the floor. "Molotok sends its regards."

He then moved his gun to point at Adam, but the boy instinctively grabbed the commando's arm and pulled him forward, shoving a knife into a seam of the armor covering his abdomen.

The perpetual gunfire ceased from the balcony and Colt listened in to the commandos' footsteps behind the walls, as they headed for the mess hall floor. "We need to go."

As they both ran past Wolf and Fox, the last remaining members of their team alive in the room, Adam ordered the couple to follow. "We have to get out of here now."

Wolf looked back at her fallen squad mates. "What about their bodies? We can't leave them."

"We have to!" barked Adam. "Now move!"

The four of them ran through the base, retracing their steps all the way to the entrance filled with bodies. Glancing over his shoulder, Fox looked back to see a wave of commandos gaining on them. "We *really* need to hurry."

After leaping through the hole they'd blown in the doors, Adam lifted his rifle and yelled to Wolf. "Get this thing moving!"

She was the first to enter the tram and headed directly towards the controls. Adam, Colt, and Fox followed behind her and turned around in the doorway, immediately opening fire at the entrance to the base.

The commandos poured into the station, fearlessly dashing towards the tram. The boys' bullets bounced off their armor, but still managed to hold the assault back long enough for the tram to start moving.

The three of them continued to hold down the triggers until their weapons clicked empty. They then fell backwards into the speeding tram, as the doors closed and they were engulfed by the tunnel's darkness.

# 16

With the high ceilings echoing his pounding footsteps, Martinez stomped through a prison corridor of mostly-empty cells. The only one occupied waited for Martinez at the far end of the hall, and he grabbed onto the bars, futilely shaking the thick, fortified iron rods back and forth. "You set them up, didn't you?!"

Inside the cell, a man with a scar across his left eye lay on a hard metal bed, staring up at the cracked concrete ceiling. He sarcastically laid his hand on his chest. "Me? Whatever are you talking about, Christopher?"

Martinez took a deep breath to calm himself, yet retained the same firm grip on the peeling bars in his hands. "You've been plotting with them all along. Communicating with them. You gave us that location because they *wanted* you to."

"You can't prove anything," said the man, shaking his head and still staring at the ceiling.

Martinez released his hold on the bars but remained standing right before them. "All this time and you still work for them don't you, Tyran?"

The man shrugged his shoulders while lying on his back, still refusing to look up at his guest. "Well, I thought your precious children could handle anything."

"You're pathetic, you know that?"

Tyran suddenly popped up off the bed, sprinted to the front of his cell, and pressed his scarred face as hard as he could between the bars. "Let me tell you about pathetic. That bitch you called a wife never once showed me that she eve knew I existed. I did *everything* for her, and she ignored me like I was nothing. *That's* pathetic. But I have to say: even after all my failures with her, the greatest moment of my life was watching your face when I slit her throat."

Martinez suddenly reached into the cell, grabbed the prisoner by his shirt, and pulled him up against the bars; but Tyran just smiled and laughed, letting his body go limp in Martinez's hands. "I know exactly what you're thinking. You want to come in here and finish what you started the day you gave me this scar. But as long as I give your superiors all the information they want ... you can't touch me. I may not get a trial while I'm in here, but at least I can still have some fun with you."

Martinez slowly relaxed his grip on Tyran's shirt. The Major parted his lips as if wanting to speak, baring his teeth, but ultimately decided to just turn and walk away.

The tap of his footsteps once again echoed off the floor, but this time they were drowned out by Tyran's bombastic laughter ,which completely filled the entire prisoner corridor. "Say hello to Vanessa for me!"

After more than two years training in the same place, Adam was still surprised by how little of The Armory he had actually seen. He hadn't even known the building had interrogation rooms; yet here he sat in one, cold, tired, and blinded by the fluorescent lights reflecting off the one-way mirror built into the side wall. He sat alone behind a desk faced by three silver chairs, trying to sit up straight despite the hours he'd been waiting for someone to arrive.

Without warning, the bland room's sole door opened and Martinez, Jason, and Christine walked into the room. After sitting down in the row of chairs, Christine and Jason each dropped a folder onto the desk, while Martinez locked eyes with Adam. "You've been relieved as squad leader."

Adam nodded, not the least bit surprised. "I expected so."

"We haven't named your replacement," added Martinez. "So you can salvage the position, if you wish to."

Adam confidently shook his head. "I failed. It's not mine anymore."

Leaning forward against the table, Christine looked at Adam with soft, sympathetic eyes. "You need to know that what happened wasn't your fault."

"I know," said Adam, once again nodding while shifting his firm gaze back and forth between the three of them. "But I still take responsibility. I know what needs to be done."

Opening the folder on the desk, Jason briefly scanned the document before looking up at Adam. "That is all. You're dismissed, Lion."

Adam stood and began walking towards the exit, but he abruptly stopped in the doorway to look back into the room. "By the way, Christine, remind me later that I owe you a pizza."

After successfully completing their first field assignment some months ago, the squad had been moved out of their barracks and into private quarters. It was an awkward transition at first, finally being able to have a moment to themselves after having spent so much time together every second of the day. Travis hadn't particularly cared for the extra privacy—except, of course, for now, when his emotions had finally become too strong to contain.

After they returned from Afghanistan with four less squad mates than they had left with, Travis retreated to his dark room and sat down on the bed, struggling to prevent the sadness from swelling in his eyes.

He hastily wiped away the tears with both hands as a voice from the shadows called to him. "Why cry, child?"

Startled, Travis looked up into the darkness. "Who's there?"

A grotesque old woman covered in rags stepped forward from the corner of the room. "You cry for your friends, don't you?"

Defensive and flustered, Travis stood up from the bed. "How'd you get in here?"

The woman slowly approached the boy with staggering steps, ignoring his question. "There's no reason to cry, Travis."

Easing his rigid stance, Travis became more confused than frightened. "You know my name?"

"I know a lot about you," she replied with a smile. "And your friend, Adam."

"Who are you?"

Having finally reached him, the woman extended a weak, wrinkly hand and brushed the side of Travis's cheek. "I'm someone who knows what needs to be done ... just like you."

# 17

The day following their disastrous mission, Adam broke away during lunch to hide in the squad's gymnasium. He sat on the floor with his back against the wall, his head hunched into his chest.

The squad as whole had known they couldn't be perfect forever. Eventually, fate would catch up with them. Failure was inevitable. But when the time came for the squad to face defeat, Adam had never imagined it would have such a devastating effect. Four of them were dead, their leader stripped of his title, and the survivors wrecked hopelessly by guilt. Adam felt as though the burden fell squarely on his shoulders and his alone.

Stuck in a downward spiral of pity, Adam was pulled out of despair by a friendly voice. "You up for a spar?"

He looked up to find Travis standing before him, wrapping his hands in athletic tape. Adam shook his head to decline the request. "I'm not in the mood."

"Come on." Travis finished wrapping his knuckles and tauntingly punched a fist into his palm. "Getting your ass kicked will make you feel better."

Adam glared at him while stretching out an open hand. "Give me the tape."

Travis smirked and grabbed Adam's hand, pulling him to his feet before tossing the tape over his shoulder at him.

After wrapping his hands, Adam threw the tape aside and the two boys took relaxed fighting stances, casually bobbing up and down while slowly shuffling around the mat.

Before their match had even really begun, Travis sought to initiate a conversation. "Still worked up over the mission?"

"No," answered Adam, hiding his true emotions while creeping forward towards his opponent. "Why? Should I be?"

Pausing their chat, each boy threw a light attack that was easily blocked by the other. Travis then picked up the discussion where they left off. "Well, you were the squad leader, and now four of us are dead. Shouldn't you feel responsible?"

"I do. But holding on to what happened isn't going to change anything. So just drop it."

Once again, the boys launched attacks that were easily blocked, then Travis resumed the dialogue. "Our first mission on foreign soil and almost half the squad doesn't make it back. That must be killing you inside."

Adam didn't respond. He kicked forward fast and hard, but Travis ducked out of the way and swept Adam's other leg, dropping him to the floor.

Furious, Adam kicked back up and charged at Travis, wildly throwing punches with both hands. "I told you to drop it!"

Adam's shout echoed through the room as the fight escalated. The two boys began moving faster and putting more force behind their punches, matching blow for blow, perfectly in sync.

Winding up, Adam swung a big hook at his opponent's head. Travis ducked out of the way and snuck under Adam's arm, grabbing him in a headlock. "Listen to me, Adam. What happened wasn't your fault."

"Yes ... it was," said Adam through gritted teeth.

Travis shook his head while speaking into Adam's ear. "No. It was *ours*."

Surprised, Adam stopped fighting against Travis's hold on him. "What?"

"You were the official squad leader, but you and I ran this team together. We're both responsible for what happened, and must hold each other accountable."

Locked in Travis's grip, Adam kept his head straight as he spoke to the sparring partner positioned behind him. "I was already punished. Martinez relieved me as squad leader."

"That's not enough, and you know it. Our brothers and sisters died out there because of our failure. Now one of us must share their fate."

Adam's eyes grew wide as he realized what his friend was after. "No ..."

He suddenly ripped himself from Travis's grasp, turning around and beginning to jab at him repeatedly. After dodging the first few punches, Travis managed to catch Adam's fists in both hands and hold them tight.

Deadlocked, the boys dug their feet into the mat as they pushed against each other, ending in a stale mate.

His face and veins tightening from the force he exerted, Adam fought with everything he had to end the standoff, but Travis was more interested in talking while simply holding his opponent at bay. "Yes, Adam. We let them down. We have to suffer the consequences."

"Shut up!" screamed Adam, continuing to push as hard as he could.

Suddenly letting up the pressure, Adam lifted his leg to kick Travis in the midsection and then tackled him to the ground. The two boys rolled around the mat in a spinning wrestling match until Travis eventually threw Adam to the side and stood up slowly, determined to finish their bout the way he intended. "I kill you or you kill me. Either way, one of us isn't leaving this room alive."

Physically, mentally, and emotionally drained, Adam slowly rose to his feet as well, and vehemently shook his head, refusing to give in to his friend's demand. "No. It doesn't have to be like this."

"Yes, it does!" snapped Travis. "Accept it."

Lowering his head, Adam let go of the guilt he'd been damming inside. It flooded his body, filling him with the anguish and grief he was so afraid of facing.

Many thoughts accompanied the pain. There was doubt, anger, and a near crippling regret. But most of all, there came a clarity unlike anything he felt before. A pure realization of the justice needed to balance their mistakes.

*Travis was right. One of them had to die.*

Raising his head to stare Travis in the eye, Adam clenched both fists at his sides and took in a deep, calming breath. He was at peace. "You're my best friend, Fox."

Travis returned the sentiment with a smile and a nod. "Mine too, Lion. Mine too."

The two fighters charged at one another and put everything they had into their battle. All their will, all their strength was focused into this one single moment. *Punch after punch. Kick after kick.* Neither one willing for even an instant to back down and accept defeat.

After several minutes of non-stop clashing, the boys could barely hold up their battered, bruised, and bloody bodies, as complete and total fatigue began to set in. They struggled to raise their fists, simply letting their heavy hands dangle at their sides.

Succumbing to exhaustion, Adam let out an animal-like snarl, while falling to his knees in pain. "You know, I never really wanted to be squad leader. I just wanted a purpose."

Staggering as well, Travis dropped down on one knee beside his weathered opponent and placed a loving hand on his shoulder. "You have one, my friend. Now change the world ..." Travis slowly stood to his feet and weakly extended his arms out to his sides, ready to accept his fate. "... 'cause you're the only one who can."

Adam looked up at Fox, a tear rolling down his swollen cheek to mix with the blood smeared across his face. "Goodbye, Travis."

Pouncing to his feet with a newfound surge of energy, Adam lifted his friend up off the ground and slammed him down hard to the mat. He then straddled on top of him, pounding on his face with both fists in a frenzy. The wet smacks of knuckles against flesh echoed around the empty gym as Adam unleashed an onslaught of pure rage onto his downed opponent.

Their blood mixed in a swirling puddle on the mat as it splashed up with every blow, into the tears pouring down Adam's cheeks. With the attacks refusing to stop, Travis's face was soon ripped open but Adam continued pounding down on the chunks of bone and mangled meat beneath him.

Across the room, Martinez walked through the door with Colt and Wolf by his side. They'd only made it a few feet in from the entrance before they spotted Adam crouched over a mutilated body, beating it into the mat.

After a brief moment of shock, Wolf wasted no time sprinting over to him. "Adam! Stop!"

While Colt froze in place, too stunned to move, Martinez followed behind her and pulled Adam off his victim, while Wolf dropped to the mat, gasping at what used to be Travis's face. "Oh my God. It's Fox."

She leaned down over the body, carefully listening for a breath and checking his pulse. Neither was there. "He's dead."

Appalled by the sheer brutality of the murder, Martinez released Adam and backed away in shock as Wolf sprinted over and began shoving Adam hard in the chest. "You killed him! Why?!"

Adam stood his ground, taking her animosity without a drop of resistance, and when the anguish became too much to bear, Wolf fell to her knees defeated, letting the flood of tears pour from her eyes. "Why did you kill our friend?"

She slowly looked up at Adam, searhing for an answer, and he gave it to her while casually unraveling the bloodstained tape from around his hands. "Because it needed to be done."

# 18

For two years, Adam had never even known this interrogation room existed, yet in the span of two days he'd now somehow found himself inside of it twice.

He sat in the same cold, metal chair, just as he had before, only this time his hands were locked in cuffs on the table.

"What were you thinking?" asked Martinez, sitting across from him.

Unlike the previous interrogation, when Jason and Christine had accompanied him, this time the Major was alone. However, their absence had no effect on Adam's mood, as he shrugged his shoulders to answer the question. "I wasn't."

"Obviously," said Martinez, enunciating every syllable to make the word hard and sharp. "You killed your own teammate!"

Adam had no response. He simply shifted his focus to the one-way glass beside him, starting at his reflection as if he could see right through it to the room behind.

His silence frustrated Martinez, who leaned back in his seat, apathetic and annoyed. "I honestly have no idea what to do with you, Lion."

"I know exactly what you're going to do with me." Turning only his head, Adam returned his gaze to the Major. "You're going to lock me in a hole somewhere and forget I exist."

The comment was meant to provoke, but Martinez nodded his head, eagerly agreeing with it. "Maybe we should. You murdered a squad mate in cold blood. There need to be consequences."

Adam's stark face continued to display zero emotion, but his eyes stared ahead, filled with life and energy. "Don't you understand? That *was* my consequence."

At a loss for words, Martinez subtly glanced over to the one-way glass, hoping like hell that the man behind it had some idea as to what should be done.

Having had enough of the conversation, Hopkins scoffed at the pair beyond the glass, before exiting the viewing room. He entered the hallway and was immediately met by Dr. Groves running towards him. "Mr. Hopkins! Mr. Hopkins! Can I please just have a moment of your time, sir!"

Rolling his eyes, Hopkins turned and began walking in the opposite direction. "This better be quick, Groves. I have a little bit of a situation I'm preoccupied with."

Having caught up, the doctor slowed down and began walking alongside him. "That's actually why I'm here. I heard about what happened and, well, I think I might have a solution to your problem, sir."

"Oh really?" asked Hopkins sarcastically. "And what would that be?"

"Give the boy to me. As a test subject."

Hopkins laughed as he continued down the hall, never breaking his stride. "Are you kidding me? The boy is supposed to be reprimanded. Not made stronger."

Groves moved up in front of Hopkins and began back-pedaling while still pleading his case. "I can assure you, sir, the procedure and tests he will undergo are far more painful than anything you can do to him. So call it corporal punishment for his actions. And if the experiment fails and the boy dies, then there's no loss. He isn't much good to his squad now that he killed one of their own, anyway."

Hopkins stopped and finally turned to give the doctor his complete, undivided attention. "And if it succeeds?"

"Well, then you will have your super-soldier. And not just any super-soldier. One that has already been thoroughly trained and is loyal to this project."

Hopkins lifted his chin ever so slightly as he weighed his options, before dropping it into an affirmative nod. "Ok, Groves. You got your test subject. Just don't make the kid any more of a monster than he already is."

# 19

Adam didn't remember how, where, or even when he fell asleep, but he firmly understood that he had woken up strapped to an operating table. Calm and composed despite the circumstances, Adam looked around and found himself in a brightly-lit laboratory, surrounded by bizarre machinery and people in white lab coats.

One man in particular walked through the crowd of working scientists and approached the table.

"Ahhh. You're finally awake. My name is Dr. Groves. And you must be Adam."

Adam turned his head, the only motion available to him, and corrected the doctor's mistake. "My name's Lion."

Groves shook his head with a smile. "Not anymore. Yesterday morning you were relieved of your position in that department and have been transferred to mine."

"Which is?" asked Adam, as if inconvenienced by the change.

"The super-soldier project."

Smiling, Adam snickered at the man's answer. "You're kidding me, right? I thought I was to be punished. This seems like a promotion."

But Groves held onto his smile as well, knowing full well what the boy was in store for. "Oh, you will be punished. The procedure will be long and painful beyond your worst imaginings."

The amusement in Adam's face faded away as he began to take his situation seriously. "And what if you turn me into a monster?"

"That won't happen. Things have changed since Stryker

volunteered. Although I can't entirely take credit for that; the improved formula came to me in a dream, believe it or not."

"A dream?" repeated Adam, skeptical of the doctor's confession.

"Yes. About an old woman, strangely enough. Anyway, according to my notes you will either become a living god or ..."

Groves's voice drifted off, forcing Adam to prompt him to finish. "Or what?"

"Or your skin will melt off and your bones will crumble while you're still alive. But you'll die several hours later."

Visualizing his potential demise, Adam's mortified gaze slowly drifted up to stare at the ceiling. "Lovely."

Groves took several steps back into the crowd of scientists, who had just finished their pre-op preparations. "Don't worry. I'm quite confident the procedure will go as planned. I put success at about ten to one odds. Give or take a percentage point or two. You ready?"

"If I say no, will it matter?" asked Adam, his eyes still fixed ahead.

Groves smiled and turned to the assistant standing by the wall. "Give it to him."

The man calmly walked over to Adam and injected the contents of a large syringe into his restrained arm, before retreating back to the wall. After a few seconds of inactivity, Adam looked around at the audience of scientists watching him, sarcastically aping confusion. "That's it?"

None of them responded, and a moment later, Adam began to notice the hairs on his arms slowly standing up on end. A tingling sensation started to spread across the edge of his skin until it grew into an intense stinging that burned his flesh like fire was running through his veins.

Tremors violently shook Adam's restrained body from side to side, and a machine hooked up to the base of the operating table clicked on, shooting jolts of electricity up and down his spine. Adam squeezed his hands tightly into fists, fighting to resist the unrelenting pain that was overwhelming him, but the tears ran uncontrollably down his face as he screamed out his horrific agony and gave in to the torment.

# PART II
## SENTIENCE

"I know not with what weapons World War III will be fought, but World War IV will be fought with sticks and stones."

Albert Einstein – Scientist

# 20

In the center of an upscale, luxurious restaurant, a stocky man in Marine dress attire enjoyed his meal alone in peaceful solitude. He was clean-shaven, well groomed, and a fairly unattractive individual who took pride in his appearance not out of vanity but discipline.

Having learned to appreciate life's frail, delicate pleasures, the man ate his steak slow and refused to look up as Hopkins approached the table and sat down. "Sorry I'm late, General."

The man responded with his eyes still fixated on his plate. "Don't apologize, Hopkins. Just give me some good news about my boy."

Hopkins leaned forward and clasped his hands onto the table. "He's exceeding our expectations. His body is responding perfectly to the designed mutations and what he can do is... well...incredible."

"Good," said the General, looking up with a mouth full of food. "And what of the subjects who followed him?"

Hopkins shook his head, delivering his account without a hint of disappointment. "Failures. Strangely, the boy's procedure has been the only one to succeed. All other participants perished during the transformation."

"Hmm." The General paused from eating, clutching the cutlery still in his hands. "Well then, I want the super soldier project's original candidates terminated and the boy to be tested in the process. Two birds with one stone. Understand?"

Hopkins nodded. "Absolutely. Would you like reports on the other projects as well, sir?"

Turning his attention back to his meal, the General stabbed the final piece of meat with his fork. "No, that won't be necessary."

Hopkins scrunched his brow, confused and hurt by the denial. "But sir—"

The General interrupted him after popping the last bit of steak in his mouth. "No buts, Hopkins. The boy is all I care about."

"With all due respect, General. The Fifth Horseman has almost ten times the power of—"

Quickly flipping the knife around in his hand, the General violently stabbed it down it down onto the tabletop, shaking the porcelain plates and drawing attention from everyone seated around them. Unconcerned with their curious eyes, the fuming General swallowed his food while staring Hopkins down, allowing the other patrons to return to their conversations before leaning forward over the table. "Listen here, you sniveling shit. That boy has become the future of war. Everything else is secondary compared to him. My partners and I have invested a lot of money on you. So don't screw it up."

Hopkins sat perfectly still, reluctant to respond with even a minute expression as the General stood from his seat while wiping the corners of his mouth with a napkin. "Now pay the bill."

The General tossed the napkin on the table and walked past Hopkins on his way out of the restaurant.

# 21

Adam had a long road of recovery after the brutal procedure that forever changed his life. Although it looked the same on the outside, his body felt in every way different than it had before. Adam had to relearn every basic task a human could perform. Walking, talking, even eating required intense focus and discipline. Almost as if he suddenly woke up in an alien's skin. Slowly but surely, as the months of training and therapy went on, the once hardened soldier returned to the point he was before.

And then he surpassed it.

Adam's strength continued to grow, lifting more and more weight until it appeared as if his muscles had no limit. He would run for miles at a dead sprint without ever getting tired, beating every speed record known to Man. And when the power inside Adam's perfectly chiseled physique became too much to contain, he found he could release it in concentrated blasts of energy. But out of every new ability Adam had discovered he was suddenly capable of, flying was by far his favorite.

In charge of the boy's super human development, Dr. Groves was proud of Adam's accomplishments but never surprised by them. He had always strove to create a specimen that fulfilled the absolute peak of human evolution and now that pinnacle was within his grasp. Almost. Adam still had a lot of training ahead of him and Groves wouldn't stop until he finished it.

Almost a year to the day after the procedure, Adam found himself in the newly constructed gym that had been specifically designed for him. With his feet merely inches above the surface, Adam casually floated off the floor for no other reason than he could. At the far end of the gym was the elevated control room window, where he could see Groves on the other side of. To test Adam's abilities, the gym had been outfitted with mechanisms to demonstrate a wide range of variables and conditions, all of which were operated from the control room. Usually the glass was polarized into a one-way mirror so that Adam couldn't see what government VIP had stopped by to check his progress. He often told Groves that he gained x-ray vision and could tell who was on the other side, a joke the doctor always took seriously.

But this time, Groves kept the window transparent as he spoke into the gym through the loudspeaker. "How are you feeling today, Adam?"

"Just fine," said Adam, still floating off the floor. "What's the morning workout for today?"

"Well, I was disappointed with the ten man combat drills from yesterday. It failed to challenge the multiple enemy tactics we worked on last week."

Adam confidently crossed his arms. "So...?"

Groves reached forward to press a button on the control panel in front of him. "So this time I'm limiting your flight capabilities."

Suddenly, the gym's high ceiling began to lower along with the control room window. Still suspended in the air, Adam curiously looked up to watch the ceiling slowly come down on top of him, stopping roughly eight feet off the floor as the control room reached the ground level.

Groves's voice then returned to the loud speaker as the door to the gym swung open, revealing a small platoon of unarmed men waiting to charge inside. "Oh, I'm also increasing the number of enemy combatants. Good luck."

The men charged ahead at full speed, and Adam remained still, quickly trying to count them all. They reached him before he had a chance to finish, forcing the teenage super soldier to flip and twirl through the air around every attack they threw at him.

The soldiers, considered some of the best in the nation's armed forces, were in awe of the boy's speed, but to Adam, his opponents moved in slow motion as he carefully dodged their sluggish punches and kicks with ease. The fight became a dance as Adam ducked under and dove through the tangled mess of arms and legs swinging his way. Whenever he saw an opening in the fight, Adam threw an attack of his own, knocking out the recipient of his fist or foot with the force of a brick wall.

As the battle slowly carried on, the number of foes left standing began to dwindle until only five fighters endured. The last remaining men fearfully held a circle around Adam, who for the first time since the fight began lowered his feet to touch the floor. The super soldier stood unafraid and relaxed with his hands casually lowered at his sides. He then slowly walked forward, stepping over the bodies of his unconscious attackers scattered throughout the gym. The circle of men moved along with him, their fists raised and waiting for their super powered opponent to make a move.

Adam stopped and scanned the men's faces until he found one, the only one, not trembling in fear. He smiled at the man and tilted his head to the side as if examining the man's bravery.

The man stared right back at him, flaring his nostrils in disgust. "What you smiling at, freak?"

Adam didn't say a word. He simply lifted his hand and shot a wave of blue energy from his palm that blasted the man square in the chest. The man flew straight backwards as if struck by a car at full speed and slammed into the opposite wall. His body then fell face first into the floor, and Adam stared at his back a moment to confirm he was still breathing.

Forcing themselves not to look at their fallen comrade, the other four men futilely attempted to remain focused and bold, but Groves's voice cut in to break their concentration. "That's enough. Dismissed."

It was clear the men were eager to leave, but they restrained themselves to merely a brisk walk towards door, trying and failing to hide their fear. As they left the gym, a medical crew entered and began tending to the moaning bodies lying around the room.

Adam ignored them as he began his departure. He only got half way, though, before Groves drew his attention towards the control room window. "Don't get full of yourself, Adam. You can always be stronger. You're not a god."

Indifferent to the doctor's comment, Adam turned and left the room, whispering under his breath. "Not yet."

# 22

Even though he had grown into something of a legend inside The Armory, Adam still ate in the same mess hall as everyone else. Everyone knew who he was and what he was capable of. For the most part they all kept their distance, either out of fear or respect.

Instead of sitting at the corner table, where his former squad spent their years, Adam always chose a seat in the center of the room. He ate his meals alone, yet still surrounded by people on every side of him. Adam enjoyed watching them walk by, curious of his power yet too hesitant to get close.

It wasn't on purpose that his schedule rarely coincided with the same times his former squad, or at least what was left of them, was also in the mess hall. When it did, Wolf was the only one he caught periodically looking over to him. He had barely said ten words to her since Travis's death. Nothing more than passing pleasantries, a quick hello or goodbye for no other reason than to avoid appearing rude.

Today though, she decided walk through the cafeteria, food tray in hand, and sit down across the table from him. "Hey."

Adam never looked up from his meal to acknowledge her presence, so Wolf pressed the issue again. "You mind if I eat with you?"

He slowly raised his head, passively annoyed by her presence. "What're you doing here?"

"I just wanted to talk to you," she said shrugging her shoulders with an innocent smile. "Thought we could catch up."

He grimaced while shaking his head. "Go back to your squad, Wolf."

Her jaw fell open, utterly stunned by his cold demeanor. "What?"

"You don't belong with me."

She froze, unable to think of a reply, and when he grew tired of waiting, Adam simply went back to eating his meal.

Wolf watched him intently for several seconds, scrutinizing his face as if he were a complete stranger. "What's happened to you, Adam?"

He answered with his eyes still focused on his plate. "Well, I think that's obvious, Sarah."

"You were never this cold before," she said while leaning over the table to get close to him. "Why are you acting like it now?"

He continued eating, ignoring the question he deemed unworthy of a response.

Wolf then stood, shaking her head in disgusted disappointment. "You know, sometimes I wish you were the one who died in that gym."

Leaving her tray on the table, she turned and exited the mess hall, passing Martinez who happened to be seated close by.

Unlike his small private quarters when he was merely a squad member, Adam now had a full-sized bedroom to call his own. It was still sparsely furnished, like much of the facility, but Adam was able to request several pieces of workout equipment he used to stay active during downtime in his training. Most of it now, such as the treadmill and weights, he had no physical use for and was nothing more than cheap exercise to occupy his mind. But there were a series a metal bars hanging from the ceiling that Adam continued to find new and interesting uses for.

With his legs wrapped around one of the bars in the center of the room, Adam hung upside down and crunched into sit-ups while holding a thick dumbbell in each hand. He was in the middle of his fifth set when he addressed a knock at the door without ever stopping. "Come in."

The door opened slowly and Martinez walked inside, stopping just inside the room. Adam paused his work out momentarily to look his guest up and down. "Oh. It's you."

He resumed his sit-ups and the Major walked deeper into the room. "You mean, 'it's you, sir.' I was your superior once. Remember, Adam?"

"But not anymore," said Adam, still crunching all the way up to the ceiling. "No one is."

Martinez stopped just far enough away so that his eyes didn't have to follow Adam's body moving up and down. "At least you can show me a little respect. I think I've earned that much after training you for two years. Or have you forgotten?"

Adam froze in the middle of a sit up with his body half crunched to look over at Martinez. "Believe me, I've tried."

In one swift motion, the boy dropped one of the weights while unhooking his feet. Before falling to the ground though, Adam's now free hand shot up and grabbed a hold of the bar. He then started performing one handed pull ups as his guest changed the subject. "I saw your conversation with Wolf this afternoon."

Adam continued the exercise with the dumbbell still in his other hand. "Eavesdropping, Martinez?"

"You can go a little easier on the girl," said the Major. "She's had feelings for you since the day you first met."

"And I told her a long time ago that those feelings are going to get her killed. You of all people should know that."

In a burst of controlled rage, Martinez pulled Adam down from the bar and slammed him up against the wall. "I don't care who you are or what you're capable of. If you bring up my wife again I will find a way to kill you."

Martinez's heated scowl was just inches from Adam's nose, but the amused boy simply laughed back in his face. "How are you going to do that, huh? By putting a gun to my head."

Calming himself down, Martinez eased off of Adam's shirt and released him from the wall. "You might be all powerful, Adam, but that doesn't make you a better person than anyone else."

Words weren't necessary for Adam to respond. The super soldier replied only with a dry, conceited smirk. The expression communicated all he needed to say.

It also ended the conversation, causing Martinez to shake his head as he turned to leave the room.

# 23

The following morning, Adam's eyes shot open to the sound of Groves's voice. "Rise and shine, Adam. Sleep well?" Lying flat on his back, Adam stretched out wide with one arm while rubbing the sleep away from his eyes with the other. "Well, I was."

"Good," said Groves, still out of the boy's line of sight.

Living in the barracks, Adam had gotten used to people invading his space while he was sleeping. Moving into his own bedroom hadn't change that. Privacy was a concept that just didn't exist inside The Armory. Especially since Adam had basically become a walking science experiment.

With his head still on the pillow, Adam rolled over in bed and spotted Groves standing by the wall, where he was filling up a thick, diamond tipped syringe with a viscous, golden liquid. "It's time for your daily shot."

Over the past year, Adam had been poked and prodded so much that he stopped keeping track of what was going in or coming out of his body. Getting a shot used to be a simple procedure, but as Adam's flesh grew tougher and more durable, the scientists were forced to experiment with different materials in order to pierce his flesh. Over time it became less of an issue as the number of injections he received slowly diminished. Now the super soldier was only getting one every morning like clockwork. Adam never put much thought into what they were for but figured maybe he should start.

He sat up off the bed and rolled up his sleeve to the shoulder. "What exactly are in these shots you keep giving me every day?"

Groves held the full syringe up to his face and, searching

for air bubbles, tapped it several times. "Just a small supplement to the procedure that allows your body to process energy more efficiently. Kind of like a vitamin."

He then walked over to the bed, stuck the needle in Adam's arm, and pushed the plunger down. "All done."

Adam jumped out of bed and pulled his arm across his body to stretch his shoulder. "Any more tests for today, Dr. Groves?"

"Nothing right now," said the doctor, returning the cap to the now empty syringe.

"I've scheduled the weight room for the morning. If you need me I'll be there."

Adam started towards the door but stopped when Groves called out to him. "I want you to know that I've been very impressed with your progress, Adam, and I'm not the only one. I've been thinking about signing off on you as field ready soon."

The boy's face subtly lit up with controlled excitement. "Really?"

"I've done all I can for you," said Groves, nodding his head. "It's time for you to get out there and do some good in the world."

Adam nodded back with an appreciative smile. He then turned and left the room as his grin grew wider.

Adam rarely entered the weight room anymore. Once it became clear that his strength had peaked at his body's maximum capacity for amplified muscle, all he had to do was maintain that mass through regular exercise. Still, Adam enjoyed lifting weights out of habit, and when he did, the super soldier made sure to secure the space all to himself. Otherwise, he tended to draw curious, leering eyes from spectators.

So Adam was surprised to find Jason and Christine already waiting for him inside the room. "What are you two doing here?"

Christine held a clipboard close to her chest and smiled upon seeing him. Jason, on the other hand, stood tall, business as usual, with his hands clasped behind his back. "We've just come to see how you're doing. That's all."

Rolling his eyes, Adam walked through the exercise

equipment over to the bench press. "You too, huh? Come to put me back in my place?"

As Jason remained where he was, Christine fell in line behind Adam, following him over to the bench as he proceeded to load the bar with as many weighted plates as it could hold. "We're not here to tell you how to act, Adam, but you're still under our observation. It's our job to monitor your progress regardless of where you're assigned in the facility."

After lying down on the bench, Adam proceeded to lift the bar and press it off his chest. "Is this progress enough for you?"

Watching him preform the exercise with ease, Christine's jaw dropped open as she tried to count all the plates on the bar, the ends of which had begun to dip and bend under strain from the weight. "That's got to be over fifteen hundred pounds."

"Well what can I say," joked Adam, smirking as he continued to pump the bar up and down. "I've been eating a lot of vegetables."

He placed the bar back on the bench press rack and sat up. "Don't you two have something better to do?"

Leaving his position on the other side of the room, Jason finally walked up to join them. "Actually, no. We're worried about your mental and emotional state since the procedure."

"I'm fine. Now are we done? I prefer to do this alone."

Disappointed, Christine reached out to hand Jason the clipboard. "I never thought all that power would go to your head. I was wrong."

She then turned and stomped her way towards the door as Jason moved up to place a hand on the boy's shoulder. "You're changing, Adam, and I don't mean physically. Having this kind of power is uncharted territory for everyone. We have no idea how it affects a human being and it's clearly turning you into a different person than you were before."

Adam shrugged his hand off and fell back down onto the bench. "I'm becoming exactly what I need to be."

He then proceeded to remove the bar from the rack and continue pressing it off his chest as Jason stood over the bench talking down to him. "Look, I know we can't stop you from acting any way you want. No one can anymore. But there's a reason Christine and I brought you here all those years ago, and it wasn't because you were some arrogant punk who cried when he didn't get his way. You were special, Adam, even before you got these powers. Just remember where you came from. That's all we ask. Remember who you really are."

Jason waited a moment for a response, but Adam ignored him as he kept pushing the bar with more force, harder and harder with every repetition. Realizing the boy had deemed their conversation over, Jason turned and approached the door. Just before he reached it though, Adam put the bar back on the rack and looked over just in time to watch Jason leave the room.

# 24

Even after he became Hopkins's most successful project at The Armory, Adam had never been invited to the man's office. Not that he particularly cared to see it. Regardless of the fact that he no longer desired it himself, Adam understood the value of privacy. So he was surprised when Hopkins summoned him to the office.

The room was located in the administrative wing at the far end of the facility. Unlike the rest of the complex, this section of the building was designed with style and class, more reminiscent of an Ivy League college campus than a government structure. Carved from wood and as large as the entire hallway, the door to Hopkins's office was the most impressive feature of all, and Adam respectfully poked his head inside rather than barge through it. "You called for me?"

Hopkins sat behind his desk at the opposite end of the room and waved the boy to approach him. "Yes, Adam. Come in."

Adam entered and took a seat in front of the desk as Hopkins re-centered his chair. "I have an assignment for you."

"Groves finally signed off on me?" asked Adam, his voice slightly elevated with excitement.

Hopkins nodded with a reserved smile. "He said you're ready and I have just the thing to get you started."

Adam sat up straight in the seat, purposefully fighting the eagerness from showing on his face. "What is it?"

"Remember that base in Afghanistan?" asked Hopkins, cheerfully. "The one where your team was ambushed? I want you to wipe it off the face of the Earth."

Whatever hint of joy remained in Adam's face instantly

faded from surprise. "Excuse me?"

Hopkins went on to dryly reiterate himself. "I want you to go back there and destroy it along with everything inside."

Confused, Adam stood slowly and began pacing behind his seat. "You want me to fly halfway across the world...kill a bunch of people...and then just blow up a building?"

Hopkins nodded with a hopeful smirk. "Should be piece of a cake for you."

Adam stopped marching back and forth across the room and turned to Hopkins, troubled by his plan. "I'm a soldier. Not an executioner."

"What's the difference?" asked Hopkins, nonchalantly shrugging his shoulders. "You've killed in that past. Even before you came here, in fact."

Ignoring the man's point, Adam shook his head, reluctant to give in. "You're treating me like a weapon. Just pointing me in a direction and pulling the trigger. I don't like it."

After pushing himself out from under his desk, Hopkins slowly walked around to place an uncharacteristically compassionate hand on Adam's shoulder. "You were always a weapon, son. We all are in some way or another. Each and every person in this facility, even myself, is nothing more than a tool with a specific purpose we live to fulfill. Some tools are stronger or more important than others. Others have to deal with the burden that comes with their role. And for you, the first super human in history, this isn't just a job we created for you, Adam. It's a life you were born for."

Adam took a breath deep breath, allowing his gaze to fall to the floor. He then looked up at Hopkins and nodded as confident and assured he could be.

Hopkins insisted that Adam depart for his mission as soon as possible, which to Hopkins meant immediately. He had the super soldier dress in what appeared to be standard issue commando fatigue pants with boots and a short-sleeved shirt. In actuality, every material he wore had been treated and tested by Groves to withstand the plasma energy Adam could dispel. Being ripped or torn was another matter entirely, though. After all, it was difficult enough making a human bulletproof without having to worry about his ensemble.

After he was dressed, Groves and Hopkins escorted Adam to The Armory's hangar bay. It wasn't nearly as large as the warehouse Martinez used to run the squad's simulations in, but the room wasn't small by any stretch of the imagination. It housed several combat choppers as well as a whole squadron of advanced fighter jets capable of a vertical takeoff and landing. But despite all that machinery, the entire room was vacant of personnel.

Adam moved to the open space in the center of the hangar and still couldn't believe he was about to embark on his first mission as a super soldier. It wasn't that he felt unprepared. He had been training for this day for almost a year. But the whole process seemed abrupt and surreal. Hopkins gave him his assignment less than an hour ago and he was already preparing to depart. No intelligence briefing. No mission parameters or objectives. Nothing.

All that considered, Groves stood next to Adam while going over a clipboard before the boy's departure. "It seems everything is physically in order."

"It better be," said Adam, staring up at the hangar's mechanical ceiling. "I've been training for a year straight."

"I would have suggested three but given your attitude I don't think I could have handled it."

Adam chuckled, taking the comment as a joke, although with Dr. Groves he couldn't know for certain if it was. The boy then looked around at the hangar, which seemed eerily creepy to be so devoid of activity. "Where are Jason and Christine? I thought following me around was all they were good for."

Hopkins's voice echoed through the empty hangar as he approached the lone soldier and scientist. "They don't know about this operation. No one does."

Over the past year, Adam's face rarely expressed concern, and in the past hour, he felt it more often than he was used to.

Sensing his soldier's worry, Hopkins went on to elaborate. "Well, that's not entirely true. A few need to know individuals are aware of it. Other than that, this mission doesn't exist. You're working off the record to take care of a personal problem some higher ups want to be handled discreetly."

His explanation only added to Adam's apprehension. "I really am just your super powered hit man, aren't I?"

"You're not getting righteous on me, are you? This hardly seems the time given all the people you've killed. Including your own friend."

Adam sighed and stared into his empty palms. "This somehow feels different, though. Like I'm not a warrior on the ground anymore. Just a bomb being dropped from the sky."

Hopkins smiled as he lightly put his hand on the super soldier's shoulder. "Adam, Adam, Adam. This is the moment you've been waiting your whole life for. As a little boy, as a soldier, and now as a super soldier. You've always wanted this power and now you have it. Go put it to use."

Groves finished writing a final note down on his clipboard and backed away. "Good to go."

Following his lead, Hopkins reached into his pocket and removed a small remote control. He clicked the device, causing the hangar's high ceiling to retract. It split down the middle as the two sides pulled away from one another, opening to the outside world above. Adam stared straight up, mesmerized by the stark blue sky as Hopkins leaned forward and whispered in his ear. "Make us proud, kid."

He then backed up to join Dr. Groves standing a fair distance away. A moment later, Adam suddenly took off, shooting straight up and disappearing into the thin cloud cover overhead.

Adam cut through the dry, desert air like a bullet, spinning and twirling the clouds around his body as he flew. At speeds only a fighter jet could match, the wind hammered his face like a brick wall, but the breeze was refreshing and crisp against his hardened skin. He hadn't felt this alive in a while, and the sensation reminded him of the first time Groves taught him how to fly.

It seemed like bizarre mysticism to Adam, the ability to harness one's energy and life force. Groves assured him, though, that many cultures acknowledged its existence.

Westerners referred to it as a soul. Indians called it prana. To the Chinese it was simply qi. Whatever its name, the procedure had exponentially increased this power within Adam, allowing him to easily harness it in new and incredible ways. Soon Groves had taught him to expel it outside his own body in the form of thrust, thus propelling him off the ground and, shortly after that, through the air. It wasn't long before he was literally floating around the facility. Now, flying was as natural to Adam as walking...if not more so.

Keeping his eye on the ever-changing countryside, Adam knew exactly when he entered Afghanistan. He had only been there once before, but the region's harsh landscape of lush fields mixed with barren mountains was a sight Adam would never forget.

He spotted the isolated village that housed the base's tram station in the distance and sped up as he began to descend. As he drew closer, though, Adam realized it was no longer a village but a compound. The area's defenses had been upgraded with high concrete walls and barbed wire fencing. From inside the small fortress, Adam spotted two small explosions that launched missiles in his direction. The projectiles rocketed straight towards him, but Adam easily rolled out of the way as the missiles flew past and detonated in his wake.

Coming to an abrupt halt in mid-air above the facility, the boy propelled himself straight down, slamming his boots onto the sand near the underground entrance he and his team once infiltrated. This time, Adam easily kicked the steel door off its hinges, startling the two guards inside and causing them to fumble their weapons. Floating off the floor, Adam zoomed into the room and easily disarmed both men before knocking them out. He then made his way down the stairwell and into the station on foot while casually firing energy blasts at any soldier unlucky enough to get caught in his path.

Once the entrance was cleared, Adam ignored the tram parked in the station and flew right past it, entering the long, dark tunnel on his way to the base. He came out of the darkness and into the next station, but Adam didn't stop there. He continued flying at full speed, slamming straight into the thick iron doorway now serving as the base's entrance. Having been newly repaired from the last time Adam was here, the door exploded once again, this time into a thousand metal shards that sprayed the base's entrance like shrapnel. Several surprised guards were instantly impaled by the sharp fragments of flying iron. Those that weren't instantly killed raised their weapons and fired randomly at the intruder.

Moving as swiftly as any human could see, Adam stole a knife from one of the men and began dancing around the entryway, dodging the bullets while slashing each and every guard as he moved. More soldiers ran into the hall firing at will, but Adam flew up and over the hail of bullets only to drop down and dismember his attackers one by one.

Dropping the knife that had served him so well, the super soldier continued on through the base, venturing from room to room and killing anyone he discovered along the way. With every second that past the massacre continued to grow. Armed with nothing but his bare hands, Adam slaughtered the base's pitiful resistance without breaking a sweat, weaving in and out of the bodies continuously falling in his path. Many soldiers turned and ran, but Adam showed no mercy. He blasted them in the back and didn't even bother to acknowledge their corpses as he stepped over them to move on.

Eventually, Adam reached the empty mess hall where his squad was ambushed a year ago. Standing in the entrance, he spotted the balcony where the heavily armed cybernetic commandos stood as they fired on top of them. He looked down at the floor that was still stained with Falcon and Ox's blood. He glanced over at the table he hid behind, now turned right side up, where he helplessly watched Hawk die right in front of his eyes.

The room was calm and silent, almost as if the memory of the battle still lingered in the air. The tranquil moment was interrupted by the light, continuous patter of feet against the concrete floor. It was a sound Adam remembered well. He recalled hearing that sound chasing after them as they escaped the base. And that's when he knew the commandos had returned.

Adam remained standing by the doorway as the they arrived. Three separate squads of commandos entered into the room: one on the balcony and two from opposite sides of the main floor. They looked exactly the same, draped in their cybernetic armor and equipped with their fancy machine guns. Adam didn't care, though. Not this time.

Merely being in the room, remembering the moment his squad mates died, filled Adam with an anger he never even knew existed. But seeing their murderers in front of him took his rage to an entirely different level. He inhaled a deep breath, trying to calm his nerves, but failed. Feeling himself slipping out of control, Adam began grinding his teeth and clenching his fists at his side. Tiny flickers of electricity started sparking off his body, causing the commandos to raise their weapons, ready to fire.

Flashing all around him, the surges of lightning continued to grow, and all at once, the commandos unleashed a hail of gunfire upon the single enemy before them. As they pulled the trigger, Adam screamed out, spiking his energy and exploding in a shockwave of fire that halted the bullets in their path. Bolts of lightning and plasma shot out around the room while a wave of flames engulfed the boy's surroundings, vaporizing the commandos in an instant. The entire building rumbled and shook from the blast as the ceiling crumbled and then finally collapsed entirely on top of him.

# 25

When Adam next opened his eyes all he could see was white. He was somehow standing even though the last thing he remembered was a ceiling collapsing on top him, but that wasn't nearly as startling as the bright, blank void he found himself in.

Perplexed by his surroundings, Adam rubbed his blurry eyes, hoping he would simply wake from a dream. He didn't. Wherever he was felt all too real and he stared out into the abyss of nothingness, realizing the horizon stretched on for eternity.

Spinning around in panicked distress, Adam soon spotted a figure dressed in black leisurely walking towards him. He squinted at the object as it slowly came into focus and gasped upon recognizing the visitor's face. "Travis?"

Seemingly back from the dead, the boy stopped in front of his old friend and smiled. "Hello, Adam."

Caught off guard, the super soldier stammered out a response. "But...you're...am I...?"

"Dead?" asked Travis, finishing the boy's question before answering it. "No. Far from it."

Adam looked around, still in awe of his endless surroundings. "Is this...am I dreaming?"

This time Travis ignored the question to initiate his own discussion. "You've been chosen, Adam."

The super soldier snapped his gaze back in his friend's direction. "Chosen? By who? For what?"

Again, Travis ignored the questions by kneeling down and waving his hand across the white floor below him. Out of nowhere, a bright, lush rose appeared beneath his palm, and

Travis picked the red flower to examine it. "Beyond earth, water, and air, life is the most delicate thing on this planet. So fragile and yet so easily broken. It's so important that it's ironic how taken for granted it is."

Baffled by the dead boy's rambling, Adam focused on something he deemed more pertinent. "Travis...what did I just do? Did I really just kill all those people...without even breaking a sweat?"

Travis stood up, shifting his attention back to his friend. "That's what you were told to do, wasn't it? Eradicate the enemy?"

"But I had no problem killing before. Why does this feel different now?"

Travis's cheeks raised slightly into a heartfelt smile. "Because now murder is no longer an act for you. It's merely a decision. That power does not come lightly, though. It's a heavy burden holding every life on the planet in your hands. But that's why you were chosen to bear it."

"Chosen?" asked Adam, growing frustrated by the cryptic answers.

"All this time you thought it was a coincidence the super soldier procedure worked for you and no one else?"

"I...I never thought about it," said Adam, his eyes darting to the floor while trying to process the information.

Travis went on to give his unsolicited explanation. "You were selected because the fate of humanity should rest in someone who understands what death truly means."

Moving up to stand side by side with his friend, Travis held the rose out in front of their faces. "People think of death as the end of life but it isn't. Life is a circle..."

Travis then lightly blew on its petals, causing the delicate flower to slowly wither and die in his grasp. "...and death is just another stop on the loop."

Frustrated with Travis's enigmatic showmanship, Adam pushed away from his friend. "Enough of this! Tell me what's going on. What happens now?"

"Only you can answer that, Adam. The people around you have given you a great opportunity. And although they have plans for you, ultimately, what you choose to do with the power is up to you."

Travis turned slowly and began walking off into the distance, leaving Adam standing alone and calling out to him. "Travis, wait!"

Travis stopped and turned around, his eyebrows curiously raised and waiting for Adam to continue, which he did after taking a long, contemplative breath. "How will I know if I chose right? What if I make a mistake?"

Travis smiled as his body began to fade into the white horizon behind him. "That's the beauty of being human, Adam. We always think we're right."

Adam's eyes shot open again and this time he saw nothing but darkness. But he felt more than he did before. A weight pressed down hard onto his body and he soon recognized where he was. Summing up his energy, Adam shot himself up through the wreckage of debris and punched a hole through the rubble he was buried under. The super soldier then soared up high over the desert floor and into the bright Afghanistan sky, never bothering to look at the obliterated base behind him.

# 26

After arriving back at The Armory, Adam was quickly shuffled from the hangar to the interrogation room that he was, unfortunately, all too familiar with. One of the facility's clueless staffers, purposefully left in the dark about everything, escorted him there. Adam didn't even bother asking him what was going.

Waiting for him in the dark interrogation room was a man he'd never seen before. Dressed in a high-ranking Naval uniform, the man sat behind a table with a folder on top of it. Adam wasn't necessarily surprised by his presence but wasn't happy to see a stranger either. "Who are you?"

"I'll be asking you some questions about your assignment in Afghanistan," said the man with a welcoming smile.

"Where are Hopkins and Dr. Groves?" asked Adam while glancing over at the one-way mirror.

The man ignored his question and gestured over to the empty chair on the other side of the table. "Please, Adam. Have a seat."

Adam obliged, although slowly, eyeing the mysterious man down as he walked over to sit in the chair. "How come I've never seen you before?"

"I don't work at this facility, and seeing as how your little field trip to Afghanistan wasn't actually 'authorized,' this isn't a formal debriefing. Just consider it a friendly chat."

Adam sternly shook his head. "I don't chat with people I don't know."

Amused by the boy's stoicism, the man smiled again. "It cost a lot of money to give you those powers. Where do you think it came from?"

"You?" asked Adam, somehow making his question sound sarcastic.

The man simultaneously nodded and shrugged his shoulders. "Among others. I'm here now to make sure it was worth it."

Previously slouched, Adam sat straight up in the chair. "I leveled the entire base in a matter of minutes. I'm sure you would consider that money well spent."

Curious, the man rubbed his chin, drastically altering his approach to the conversation with a more inquisitive tone. "Did you experience any personal connection to the location in terms of feelings or emotions? Or was it strictly a tactical operation?"

Adam stared at the man sideways, almost annoyed by the question. "I lost teammates at that place. Of course it brought back memories."

"And how did those memories make you feel? Sad? Angry? Nostalgic?"

Growingly irritated, Adam leaned forward onto the table, flaring his nostrils in contempt. "I felt...nothing."

"Nothing? Not a single thought was going through you head?"

"No."

After nodding oddly, the man casually opened up the folder and began scanning a document inside. "It says here you killed your first human being when you were fourteen."

For the first time in years, images of that day rushed back into Adam's mind. He saw flashes of himself standing over the boy's pummeled face, staring down at his own blood soaked hands. For a moment, Adam tried to recall the boy's name before realizing he never even knew it.

"Yes," said Adam, eventually confirming the man's statement.

The man then went on as his eyes continued to scan the page. "And as I mentioned earlier, you were originally assigned to the super soldier project because of a murder involving your old squad mate."

Adam experienced another flash of his bloody fists. This time when he looked down he saw Travis's corpse staring back at him. It wasn't a memory he regretted but one he would rather not dwell on.

"What are you getting at?" Adam finally asked, annoyed.

The man returned the piece of paper in his hands to the table. "How many men have you killed before the procedure?"

"As a soldier of this country? A lot," Adam responded quickly.

"And since then?"

Adam wanted to answer again as rapidly as he could but the words struggled to come out. "I've done nothing but train with my powers since I received them."

"So none?" asked the man for clarification.

Adam shook his head. "Except for this first mission. No."

The man looked at Adam curiously. "I sense a tone in your voice."

"I just don't understand the point of all this."

Returning his attention to the folder, the man turned around the next document inside and pushed it across the table closer to Adam. It was a picture of the super soldier taken only moments ago from a surveillance camera in the hangar. The photo was zoomed in on Adam's troubled face, staring fixed at the floor.

Adam continued to examine the portrait as the man spoke. "You told me you felt nothing after killing all those people today, yet this looks like someone who has a lot on his mind, don't you think?"

After tossing the photograph aside, Adam directed his ire back at the man seated across from him. "It's just...every life I've taken before was personal. It was direct. I saw a target and pulled the trigger. Now...now I am the trigger."

"Are you okay with that?" asked the man, appearing only slightly interested in Adam's response.

Adam straightened up in his seat and wiped any hint of emotion from his face. "I did what I was supposed to."

The man slyly shook his head. "That's not what I asked."

Apathetic to his answer, Adam indifferently shrugged his shoulders. "I just didn't think the first mission with my powers would be to annihilate hundreds of people."

The man closed the folder with another smile, but unlike

before, his expression now reeked of condescension. "Well, what did you think they would be used for?"

Lowering his gaze, now filled with unexpected doubt, Adam just shook his head while staring at the bland table in front of him. "I...I don't know."

Despite the bad memories of the place, Wolf often found solace in her squad's gymnasium. There was an odd tranquility that came with the violence of striking a heavy bag. Wolf discovered that lost in a fury of punches and kicks she could become free and clear of any baggage weighing down her mind.

But as she turned a corner into the gymnasium and found Adam standing in the corner she could feel the stress spiking inside her. It wasn't just any corner. It was the corner he and Travis fought when Adam pummeled him into oblivion. The super soldier stood with his back to the entrance, idly staring at the mat underneath his feet.

Wolf expected her back to slump in disappointment upon spotting them. Instead, her shoulders remained tense, tight, and rigid. "You've got some nerve."

Adam still didn't turn around to face her. He remained still, his head drooped and his gaze lowered.

Frustrated by his silence, Wolf stomped across the room to approach him. "You tell me to get lost. That I have no business being around you. And then you show up here? In this room of all places?"

She stopped behind him and waited again for a response that never came.

"Damn it, Adam," she snapped. "Just say something!"

"You were right," he finally muttered, just loud enough for her to hear him.

"Right about what?" asked Wolf, still staring at his back.

Adam answered under his breath. "I was the one who should've died that day."

It wasn't the confession Wolf was expecting, but she didn't allow herself to feel grateful for it. "If you're looking for some shoulder to cry on then—"

Adam cut the girl off by finally turning around to face

her. "I've spent half my life feeling weak and the other half pretending to be strong. Now I have all this power and not a damn clue what to do with it."

Wolf inhaled deeply and stared into Adam's eyes. They weren't the strong, confident eyes she was used to seeing but rather filled with uncertainty and worry.

It was an expression further reflected as Adam lowered his head. "Travis would've known, though. He wouldn't have doubted himself for a second."

"But he's not here anymore," said Wolf, sharpening her words into condemnation. "You took him for us."

"I didn't want to," replied Adam, looking back up to her. "But Travis knew what was coming. I don't know how or why, but he sacrificed himself to put me on this path. So that when the time came I could figure out what this power was for."

"Which is?" asked Wolf, refusing to allow her voice to soften.

Adam shook his head and gently reached out to her. "I don't know yet. But I'm afraid of what I might find out alone."

Wolf reacted scornfully by pulling her hand away and taking a step back. "No. You don't get to undo everything that's happened."

Adam took a step forward, closing the gap Wolf created between them. "I don't want to, Sarah. What I want to know is what comes next. How to move forward when every bone in my body is screaming at me to stand still."

Wolf looked into Adam's eyes once more and saw a familiar vulnerability. Not familiar to her. She had never known the boy to waver in his conviction. But the insecurity etched into Adam's face didn't seem new to him. Almost as if that trepidation was once all he ever knew.

Wolf wouldn't be fooled by it, though. Adam was still responsible for too much pain to be forgiven.

"Well, you've gotten this far by yourself," she said, uncaringly shrugging her shoulders as she turned to walk away. "What's a little further?"

Wolf wanted to turn around, to look back over her shoulder at him, but she forced her eyes ahead while exiting the gymnasium doors and disappearing out of sight.

# 27

Vanessa Stryker's voice echoed loudly down the hall as Hopkins approached the laboratory in the distance. "This is bullshit! No! I will not settle down! I was told three Goddamn years ago this would be over. Don't give me that. You haven't even begun to—"

Hopkins immediately cut her off as he turned into the lab, a stark white clean room filled with glassware and computerized equipment. "What's going on here?"

With his assistants lining the outskirts of the room, Groves stood across from Vanessa, who turned her fuming ire at the newest person to walk through the door. "Hopkins! You're closing the funding for Robert's cure!?"

"Not closing," he said, approaching her with his arms slightly raised to display his innocence. "Just reallocating the budget. The men in charge need to move some funds elsewhere, but we're not giving up hope. Are we, doctor?"

Groves rapidly nodded his head in agreement. "That's correct. We're doing all we can, Mrs. Stryker."

Vanessa was less than swayed by his appeal and walked forward to leave the room. "You're full of crap, Hopkins. I hope you rot in hell."

"However…" Hopkins stepped in front of her path, halting her departure. "If you were to do a little favor for me I'm sure something could be arranged."

Vanessa sat back in her stance and crossed her arms annoyed. "You're extorting me with my husband's life?"

"Not at all," Hopkins responded, nodding his head with a smirk. "Your help would just allow me to keep some of our resources on Robert's case."

"So you want me to do your dirty work?"

Hopkins tilted his head to the side, doing his best to appear offended. "Vanessa, do you really think so little of me?"

Vanessa remained in the same position, refusing to answer the man's question and forcing him deliver his offer. "Last week Adam completed a crash course in advanced sword fighting techniques. Don't ask me why, but it was part of his training regiment. If you were to spar with him, test out his skills some, I would greatly appreciate it."

She shrugged her shoulders, skeptical of the request. "That's it? Just spar with the boy?"

He nodded with a smile. "You scratch my back and I'll scratch yours."

She lifted a firm finger and dug it into Hopkins's chest. "You better not be lying to me."

"You have my word," he said, nodding confidently.

She then used the same finger to push him out of her way before leaving the room. With the show over, the lab assistants went back to work as Groves moved up to stand alongside his boss. "That woman is becoming a problem."

"Don't worry, doctor," responded Hopkins, stepping forward to exit the room as well. "I'm taking care of it."

Hopkins approached Adam's room and reached for the doorknob when it suddenly turned on its own. The door opened slowly and he was surprised by the face there to greet him. "Christine. I wasn't expecting you here."

She had a look of complete scorn and the tone in her voice was equally as sharp. "Where has he been?"

Hopkins assumed he heard her anger correctly but genuinely had no idea where it was coming from. "Excuse me?"

"Adam left The Armory, but he won't tell us where he went."

Although he had hoped to avoid such a confrontation, Hopkins had nothing to hide and held his head high to justify his action. "Adam's a soldier. He was just following orders."

She moved in closer to throw her attitude right in his face. "What about my orders? Jason and I are supposed to track his movements. Follow his progress. How can we do that if we're left in the dark about what he's doing?"

Christine was looking to shame him, but Hopkins owned her condemnation by shrugging his shoulders with an indifferent grimace. "Sorry. But it's above your pay grade."

"You're an asshole," she chided through an ugly scowl.

The two of them silently stared at each other for several seconds before Adam called out from inside the room. "It's over, Christine. What's done is done."

"You're really going to take his side on this?" she asked hesitantly, turning to face the boy seated up on his bed.

Adam stared blankly at her without nodding or shaking his head. "There are no sides here. Just what we can or can't accept. So just let him in and move on."

Hopkins moved past Christine to enter the room and was subjected to the stare from her ferocious eyes up until the moment he shut the door in her face. He then turned his attention around to Adam. "Recent satellite imagery shows a giant hole where the underground base used to be located. Well done."

Adam subtly raised his chin. "It was like you said. Piece of cake."

Hopkins took several steps forward to approach the bed. "That's good to hear. Because the day's not over yet. You still have to take part in a little sparring session I arranged with Vanessa Stryker."

"You want me to kill her, don't you?" asked Adam, flatly.

The profound question caught Hopkins by surprise and he scrambled to look offended. "Whatever would make you think—"

"You can't hide it from me," interrupted Adam, shaking his head. "The lie is all over your face."

Wiping away his faux shock, Hopkins stood tall and adjusted his demeanor. "How did you know?"

Adam stood up off the bed. "It doesn't matter. I'll do it, but don't come in here trying to manipulate me."

"And Martinez, as well?" asked Hopkins.

Adam's back straightened at the unexpected request, but his face never flinched. "You have no conscience, do you?"

Hopkins innocently shrugged with a guilty smirk. "I'm just trying to clean a little house. And since you did such a wonderful job in Afghanistan I figured why not let you help."

"I thought you said I'm not your super human hit man?" asked Adam, his face remaining unchanged.

Hopkins reached out and placed a soft, caring hand on Adam's shoulder. "Which is why I want to make sure you're okay with this?"

The super soldier then shrugged off the overtly forced gesture of compassion before exiting the room. "It doesn't matter either way."

# 28

Although he had heard about Adam's new training gym, Martinez had yet to actually see it for himself. He didn't necessarily desire to, either. These days, the Major had a very simple role at The Armory, managing the squadron he trained as its commanding officer. So it concerned him that he was being summoned to the gym's control center.

Inside he found several technicians working at isolated stations around the room, but he ignored them to approach Hopkins waiting for him by a mirror. "Sir, I was told you wanted me here."

"Yes," Hopkins said to the Major. "You trained Adam in sword combat, did you not?"

Martinez nodded suspiciously. "I did. Years ago. But what does that have to do with anything?"

"I wanted to see if you noticed any improvement."

Hopkins reached forward to press a button on the wall below the mirror, causing it to morph into a transparent piece of glass. The change drew Martinez's attention and he looked through it to find Adam and Vanessa stretching in the training room below. "What is this?"

"Vanessa's the best sword fighter I know," noted Hopkins while also looking through the glass. "I'm having her test the boy's skill and want you to evaluate his progress. Don't worry. I told him to play fair."

Martinez shook his head and turned his attention back to the man beside him. "Adam hates me. He won't fight if he knows I'm here."

Hopkins smirked with his eyes still dead ahead. "The glass is one-way. They can't see in. Just relax and watch."

The major let out an uncomfortable sigh and waited a moment before focusing once again through the glass.

In the gym below the control room, Adam and Vanessa slowly approached one other with katana swords in hand. Vanessa's outfit consisted of a helmet, chest plate, and pads on her limbs. It was all standard equipment to protect her during the match, none of which Adam needed or desired to wear. Each of them stopped about ten paces away, but while Vanessa took a fighting stance ready to begin, Adam stood casually with his weapon lowered at his side.

He then proceeded to flip the sword around and stab it into the gym floor before approaching his opponent unarmed. "I know we've only spoken a couple times and we don't know each other all that well, but I really am sorry about what happened to your husband. From what I hear he was a good soldier and an even better man. It would have been an honor to fight alongside him."

Vanessa relaxed her stance but kept her sword raised as the boy continued walking towards her. "Thank you, Adam. But what are you doing?"

Looking away from the glass, Martinez turned to Hopkins. "What's going on?"

Although less concerned than the Major, Hopkins held a look of genuine puzzlement as he stared into the room. "I have no idea."

Adam continued approaching her, taking each step as slowly as possible. "I need to know before we do this: after what he's become, do you still love him?"

Vanessa shook her head while finally lowering the sword to her side. "Adam, I don't know what—"

"Just answer the question," Adam demanded, stopping right in front of her.

"Yes, of course."

"What if I told you that you had the chance to save him? All you had to do was kill me."

Confused, Vanessa scrunched her brow. "What's this about, Adam?"

He reached out and casually took the sword from her hand. "Hopkins wanted me to strike you down during our match and play it off like an accident."

Infuriated by the confession, Vanessa looked up at the one-way glass, clenching her teeth. "I knew he was up to something."

Adam then held the sword up sideways and ran his other hand across the blade, infusing its metal with a burning energy that caused it to glow in a fiery red. "But it's not going to happen like that. You deserve better, so I'm going to fight you fair. No powers. Just us. Either I kill you or you kill me."

"Why?" Vanessa questioned.

Adam flipped the sword around, extending the handle back for Vanessa to grab. "All the other candidates are gone. If I die, Hopkins will have no choice but to cure your husband to continue the project."

"No," she said, not yet taking back the enhanced sword. "I meant why would you kill me for him?"

"Not for him," corrected Adam. "For me."

She again scrunched her brow confused. "I don't understand."

"You don't have to. All you need to understand is that only one of us is leaving this room alive."

She took a deep breath, still refusing to retrieve the sword. "It doesn't have to be like this. We can work together and come up with a better way."

"Don't mistake my respect for friendship. We are not on the same side here and I can end your life in an instant if I truly wanted to. So choose your next words wisely because I will not be making this offer again."

Vanessa glared at him for a moment, weighing every one of her grim options, before finally placing her hand back on the weapon. "Fine. I'll do it."

Martinez anxiously watched through the glass as Vanessa began removing the protective gear from her body. "What are they doing? I know you know."

Hopkins innocently shrugged his shoulders. "I already told you I don't."

In a burst of anger, Martinez grabbed Hopkins by the collar and pulled him in close. "Don't lie to me!"

With their faces just inches apart, Hopkins stared the Major down, completely unafraid. "Whether I am or not doesn't matter. Whatever they're up to is out of your control. So all you can do is watch and hope for the best."

Realizing he was right, the anger slowly drained from Martinez's face. He then released his grip on Hopkins's shirt and turned his attention back to the gym.

Adam pulled the impaled sword from the gym floor and took a fighting stance opposite Vanessa. The two warriors eyed each other down until Vanessa moved first, lifting her glowing sword and then slashing from overhead. The steel edges connected for only an instant before she struck again. Adam parried as he had done before and launched a weak counter, which Vanessa easily avoided. The fighters exchanged moves one after the other as they gracefully danced around the room. Even without the use of his super speed, Adam was able to nimbly dodge her attacks while Vanessa's blade flowed as a perfect extension of her body.

Without pause, Vanessa relentlessly attacked high and low, clashing their swords back and forth like lighting. Her onslaught kept Adam constantly on the defensive and somehow found an opening, slicing her enhanced blade across his bicep. It was the first time Adam had felt physical pain in a long while. It had been even longer since he had seen his own blood. He couldn't stop and reflect on it though, as his opponent never let up for an instant.

Breaking her chain of attack, Vanessa suddenly stepped back and quickly lunged forward. Reacting on instinct, Adam swiftly spun out of the way, around Vanessa's side, and slid his blade straight into her back. The tip of the sword pushed through Vanessa's chest, causing a shot of blood to spew from her mouth. Coughing in agony, she looked down at the blade sticking out of her and went limp, causing the weapon to slide out of her hand. Adam held her there for a moment, lifeless and at his mercy, before dropping the woman to her knees and slowly removing the sword from her body.

"Vanessa!" screamed Martinez, pounding the window in horrified shock.

The noise immediately drew Adam's attention. In one swift motion, the boy spun around, flicking his wrist and letting the sword fly towards the shaking glass. A moment later, the sharp blade pierced the window and slid straight through Martinez's head, killing him instantly.

Startled by the sudden attack, Hopkins stumbled backwards before regaining his composure and realizing Martinez was dead. "Oh, Adam."

The Major's body went limp but remained upright, dangling from the sword still imbedded into the glass. Blood drenched the entire blade sticking out the back of his head and the thick liquid began dripping to the control room floor. Curious at the unusual sight, Hopkins walked up and began examining the corpse with a smile. "Now you've outdone yourself."

On the other side of the glass, another trickle of blood seeped through the crack, passed the sword's handle, and started streaming down the mirror. Adam's expression didn't change after noticing the ooze of blood. He emotionlessly turned to leave when he felt a firm hand grab ahold of his ankle. Adam looked down and found Vanessa staring up at him.

"If you ever see Robert," she said, her voice weak and raspy. "I'm talking about my husband. Not the thing he is now...tell him I'm sorry...and that I tried."

Even in her final moments, with her face drained of vitality, Vanessa's eyes still radiated with adoration. That expression, the desperation of Vanessa's love, evoked a feeling in Adam he had once fought to ignore. Now he didn't see a point in denying its existence.

The boy waited a moment longer, watching as the last vestige of life left Vanessa's body. He then pulled his leg from her grasp and hurried towards the exit.

# 29

Adam turned a corner to enter his squad's old dormitory and found Wolf walking away from him half way down the hall.

"Sarah!" he yelled out while jogging to catch up to her. "Wait!"

Shaking her head, she let out a deep sigh as she continued moving forward. "I don't have time for your mind games, Adam. You wanted me to leave you alone. Now I'm asking you to do the same."

He caught up and began following close behind her. "Just listen to me for a second."

She refused to turn around, continuing on down the hall. "We already talked about this. I want nothing to do with you anymore."

"Please. I only have one more thing to say and then I'll be gone. I promise."

She reached her room and looked up at Adam, silently wondering what this was all about. Finally breaking eye contact, she looked down the hall both ways before opening up the door. "Fine. Just come in. I don't want anyone to see you here."

She entered the room and Adam followed behind her. He then shut the door and took a slow, deep breath, preparing his nerves before speaking. "I wasn't honest with you."

Wolf turned and sat down on her bed. "Is this two confessions in one day? Wow. I must have won the lottery."

"A long time ago I told you I didn't trust you because you had feelings for me," Adam explained. "I lied. It wasn't that I couldn't trust you. It's that I couldn't trust myself."

Unsure as to how she felt about the conversation, Wolf physically squirmed in her seat. "What are you talking about?"

"I felt something for you, too." Adam began approaching her slowly. "I tried to ignore the knot in my stomach or even pretend it wasn't there. I got so good at pretending I didn't even care that I fooled myself into living a lie."

"Why would you do that?"

"Because of who we are...because of what we were trained to be I was scared of what those feelings meant. Scared of what they could lead to."

"And you're not anymore?" she asked skeptically.

Having finally reached her, Adam took her hand and dropped down to a knee. "Oh, I'm terrified. And you know what? It feels great. I haven't been scared like this in a long time. It makes me feel alive. Like a person and not just some powerful weapon ready to be deployed. You make me feel this way, Sarah. You. And I'm ashamed for what it's taken me to realize that."

Wolf looked away while shaking her head, fighting the urge to lower her guard. "Adam...I don't—"

He cut her off by lifting a hand and gently running his fingertips down the side of her face. "I'm sorry. I should've never made such beautiful eyes cry."

His soft touched caused Wolf to close her eyes, her lips beginning to quiver. "What are you saying?"

"I'm saying I love you. I always have."

She opened her eyes and smiled. "I...I love you, too."

He slowly moved up and pressed his lips firmly against hers. The two teens held their kiss in place, enjoying the moment they both had waited so long to embrace. Adam then moved forward even more, wrapping his arms around the girl completely and bringing her in close as they fell onto the bed.

"Time to tie up the loose ends," muttered Hopkins under his breath.

Hopkins punched a code into the keypad on the wall and the steel door in front of him shot open. He then entered into the dark room and stopped beside the link of a giant chain lying on the floor. "Wake up, Stryker."

Two beady, red eyes emerged from the darkness, lighting up the area around them.

"I need to speak to you," Hopkins said to the large, primal pupils. "Something's happened to Vanessa." The ground trembled as the lumbering beast stood off the floor and Hopkins went on. "I'm sorry, but she was killed by a boy."

Grunts and growls echoed around the room as the chain shook and pulled against the wall. Hopkins backed up towards the door, completely unafraid of the stirring fiend. "His name is Adam Judson. He's a super soldier. What you signed up to be. What you were supposed to become. Instead, it made you what you are now."

The snarling monster threw himself around the room in a fit of rage, snapping the chain in two. Hopkins stopped in the hallway but kept peering into the room, watching the beast work himself into a frenzy. "Vanessa was the only one who cared about you and now she's gone. That boy took the only thing you have worth living for, Stryker. Now...what are you going to do about it?"

Pressing a button on the keypad, Hopkins shut the door with a smile on his face. He then listened from the hall as Stryker unleashed a horrific roar while tearing apart his cell.

# 30

Adam's eyes opened to the sight of Wolf sleeping soundly on the pillow beside him. It was a strange feeling to wake up in a state of happiness. He had experienced so little joy in his life that the sensation was almost alien to him, but the fact that he couldn't stop smiling was all Adam cared about.

He stood and quietly put on his clothes, careful not to wake the girl from her peaceful slumber. He then leaned over the bed to place a soft kiss on her forehead. The gentle touch of his lips caused Wolf to roll over, cuddling up to the sheets while nuzzling her head into the pillow. Still holding onto the same wide smile, Adam watched her sleep for a moment longer and then silently left the room.

Laughing to himself, the giddy boy strolled down the hall with his head held high. No matter how hard he tried, Adam just couldn't seem to wipe the smile from his face. For the first time in his life he actually caught himself daydreaming about the future, optimistically wondering what tomorrow might bring.

Every one of those thoughts were then shattered when Stryker suddenly came crashing through the wall beside him.

In an instant, the monster emerged from the wall, grabbed Adam by the torso, and slammed him into the opposite side of the corridor. The beast didn't stop there, though. He kept on running straight through The Armory, smashing Adam into every wall in their path.

The boy was helpless, held immobile like a doll in Stryker's claw-like hand. After finally being able to wiggle his arm free, Adam fired a blast of energy at the monster's head, which stopped his rampage through the facility in the middle of the mess hall. Stryker dropped Adam to the floor and let off an inhuman howl, terrifying the people in the mess hall too frightened to run for their lives.

Adam rose to his feet and stared the monster in his crimson, devilish eyes as he grumbled out a single word. "Vaaaaaneeeessssssaaa."

Drool dribbled out from between the creature's twisted fangs as he snarled at the boy before him, but Adam refused to look away, standing firm with his clothes in tatters. "I'm sorry about your wife. I really am. But her death was inevitable."

"Diiiiiiiiiiieeeeeeeeeee!!!" roared Stryker, pulling back his claw.

He swiped forward but Adam easily jumped out of the way. The beast followed up with another attack, but his lumbering movements were too slow to hit the speedy super soldier. Adam ducked and dodged every slash of Stryker's claw, but the relentless brute left no opening for Adam to strike back. With what little time he had, Adam quickly fired short bursts of energy into the monster's torso, but Stryker barely flinched before continuing his onslaught.

In an attempt to gain the upper hand, Adam darted over the creature's head, but Stryker pounced straight up, catching Adam and slamming him through the ceiling. Again, the couple charged ahead, crashing through several layers of ceiling before smashing through a thick layer of rock and up through the surface. Tangled as one, the two of them popped up through the dry air and then broke free from one another's grasp, falling hard onto the cracked desert earth.

The scorching sun beamed down onto Adam as he stumbled to his feet, covered in blood and his clothes ripped to shreds. He surveyed his soundings and saw nothing in every direction but the barren desert along the horizon.

Behind him, Stryker let out a monstrous roar, ready for round two, and Adam turned to face him with his hands lowered at his sides. "It's not too late, Stryker. You're free. No more chains and no more cages. All you have to do is turn and walk away."

"Yoooooouuuuuuuu must diiiiiiiiiieee."

"Fine," said Adam, raising his fists. "Have it your way."

The boy flew forward at full speed and slammed into the monster's chest. Stryker soared backward before coming to a stop by digging his clawed feet into the dry ground under him.

Adam flew forward again, buzzing around Stryker's hulkish body as the creature futilely swiped at him like an insect. Floating through the air, Adam landed several kicks and punches before flying away unharmed. Annoyed by the boy's hit and run tactics, Stryker let out an aggravated roar while maniacally swinging his arms around in a frustrated rage.

Utilizing the distraction, Adam landed behind the beast and brought the heels of his hands together to focus his energy. "Say hello to your wife."

Stryker turned around just as Adam unleashed a wave of energy from his palms at full force. The creature lowered his shoulder into the blast and fought it back by digging his talons into the ground.

In a tense standoff, the two sides continued to fight each other back, neither one willing to give in or let up. Surprised by the monster's resistance, Adam screamed while pushing harder to overpower him. The veins on his arms and neck began rise and bulge from the strain as the taxed boy pumped more energy, everything he had, into the blast.

While clenching his teeth to fight past the pain, blood trickled out from Adam's nose, but he ignored it, focusing solely on the fact that Stryker's mutant body began to vaporize into the beam. As he was literally disintegrating into nothingness, the creature let out a horrific shrill of agony but continued to fight, unable to control the fact that his body was fading away until there was nothing left but dust.

Once every bit of Stryker had vanished from existence, Adam released the wave of energy, allowing it to dissipate through the air. The exhausted boy then stumbled forward, swaying back and forth before passing out onto the desert floor.

# 31

Adam's eyes abruptly shot open as he gasped for life. After several short, erratic breaths, the boy calmed himself enough to realize his whole body ached. He tried to sit up when a sharp soreness pinched him in the ribs. He fought through the pain only to realize a series of green shackles were tying him down onto a cold, metal slab. Adam pulled on the chains but the strange metal wouldn't break. It had nullified his powers, a feat which he didn't even know was possible. His eyes slowly blinked as he scanned his surroundings. He was in what appeared to be a dimly lit prison cell surrounded by bars.

Adam never thought he could feel so helpless as a super soldier and grew nervous as he suddenly spotted vague movement in a dark corner of the cramped room. "Who...who's there?"

"Hello, Adam," said a hoarse, gravely voice he didn't recognize. "I've heard much about you."

Adam squinted, trying to make out a face or a shape. "Do I know you?"

The more he stared the more Adam's eyes adjusted to sense the outline of a man speaking to him. "You know of me."

"Turn the lights on," Adam demanded with the faint hint of fear in his voice.

"No," said the man. "I actually prefer the darkness after living in it for so long."

Again, Adam tried to move but the strange shackles wouldn't budge. "Who...who are you?"

The man stayed in place, watching Adam struggle to break himself free. "I came to say thank you for taking care of my former squad mates. You've saved me the trouble of killing them myself."

Adam stopped futilely fighting against his restraints and peered into the darkness, finally realizing the identity of his mysterious visitor. "Tyran?"

Adam could see the silhouette nod his head. "Yes, Adam. I'm here to return the favor."

"What's going on?" asked Adam, both curious and confused by the man's presence.

Emerging from the darkness, Tyran walked over to the chains and used a rusty, green key to unlock them from Adam's wrists. "You have the power of a god, Adam, and gods aren't meant to be chained let alone take orders from men in their ivory towers. You have a bigger calling. You need to be out there in the world and amongst its people to truly understand the purpose of your gifts."

Now free from his shackles, Adam attempted to sit up again and grunted in pain. "I don't know if—"

Tyran leaned in even closer to stop the boy from moving, and for the first time Adam could see the deep scar across his face. "Please don't get up. You need your rest for what comes next."

Adam looked at him curiously. "And what's that?"

"Exactly what you want," said Tyran with a grizzly smile. "We're going to change the world."

# 32

Adam woke again, this time to the sound of a loud alarm blaring through his skull. He shot up off the metal slab to find his dark prison cell flooded with flashing red lights. The cell door was wide open with the green shackles lying unlocked on the floor. He cautiously walked through the door and up the stairs, entering a hallway filled with people looking around confused.

Adam then moved through the crowd and unknowingly past Jason staring at him curiously. "Adam…?"

The boy ventured on down the hall, ignoring the throngs of people in his path. Jason took off after him, surprising Christine who had been standing beside him. "Jason, where are you going?"

After rounding several corners, Adam entered one of The Armory's many security centers. The room was filled with attendants, all scanning a huge wall of security monitors that displayed almost every hallway in the building. Two armed soldiers stood guard on either side of the room while Hopkins anxiously positioned himself behind the attendants. "I want every corner of this complex searched. I'm not letting him leave here with those notes."

As his eyes drifted around the room, one of the guards noticed Adam standing by the doorway and quickly lifted his weapon to aim it at him. "Freeze!"

The other soldier followed suit, but Adam ignored them both to approach Hopkins. "What's going on?"

Without turning around, Hopkins scoffed and answered the boy with his back to him. "What's it look like? We're in the middle of a breakout. First a monstrous bio-experiment, then a traitor, and now…apparently you."

Jason and Christine ran into the room and stopped behind Adam as he stared at Hopkins confused. "Me?"

Hopkins turned around slowly. "You've killed two high ranking employees of this facility."

He then leaned forward and whispered into Adam's face. "I could've written off Vanessa as an accident, but I can't protect you for killing Martinez. When I asked you to kill him I didn't mean now. Looks like you're going to rot in a cell for the rest of your—"

Adam swiftly grabbed Hopkins by his throat and lifted him up off the ground. The soldiers took a unified march forward with their weapons at the ready but held from firing as Christine moved in their way. "Adam, stop!"

Holding out his hands, Jason slowly walked up to the boy, talking softly to calm him down. "Hopkins isn't not worth it, Adam. Just put him down and we'll talk about this."

But Adam ignored them both, speaking directly to his victim as he squeezed his throat. "You mentioned some notes. What were you talking about?"

Clawing at Adam's hand around his neck, Hopkins struggled to answer in a raspy voice. "It's none of your business."

Adam punched Hopkins in the stomach, causing the soldiers to take another joint step forward. Before they had a chance to shoot though, Adam fired two energy blasts from his other hand, easily knocking away the soldiers' weapons.

Jason and Christine flinched from the attack and Adam turned his attention back to Hopkins. "Tell me."

With his feet helplessly dangling off the floor, Hopkins answered in between weak gasps for air. "Tyran. He took Groves's notes."

"What?" asked Adam, more shocked than confused.

"Intelligence on the super soldier project. Serum, formulas, blueprints. It's all gone."

Processing the information, Adam's gaze fell to the floor as a dreadful hush filled the room.

Sarah then curiously walked through the doorway and broke the silence. "Adam…?"

He turned to her, dropping his hostage to the floor in the

process. Hopkins fell backwards and coughed several times before regaining his ability to speak. "Adam Judson, you're under arrest and are to be held without trial for the murders of Vanessa Stryker and Christopher Martinez."

Adam looked over to Jason and Christine, who both shook their heads in disbelief as Hopkins slowly stood to his feet. "Don't look at them. They can't help you."

Wolf stepped forward, still confused and taking in the baffling scene she walked in on. "Is it true?"

Adam nodded silently and Wolf's face grew wide in appalled shock. "Why would you do such a thing?"

Adam answered in a soft, placid voice. "Because...they are better off that way."

Wolf continued to stare at him, unable to comprehend what she was hearing or stop a single tear from running down her cheek. "Adam, what are you talking about? You just admitted to murder like it was nothing. Are you insane? Didn't you learn anything from Travis?"

Adam looked at her with an unfortunate grimace. "I learned that death is our connection to life. That our fleeting moments of happiness might give meaning to the pain, but it's only a mask for the despair inside each and every one of us."

Wolf shook her head, her face tightening to hold back the tears swelling in her eyes. "So telling me you loved me..."

She let her voice trail off, reluctant to bring up the memory given the betrayal burning her up inside, so she asked the one question on everyone's mind. "How could anyone think that way?"

Adam took a deep breath and held his head up high with conviction. "I didn't think it. I felt it. I felt their sorrow. Their anguish. Their heartache. And now it's gone. Because of me they hurt no more. I helped them."

Wolf shook her head side to side, utterly baffled by the boy's answer. "You really don't believe that, do you?"

With a reluctant grimace, Adam turned away from her to face the wall. "I...I need to go."

She reached out to him with a quick step forward. "No, Adam. Don't—!"

"Goodbye," he said, interrupting her one last time.

Adam shot straight up through the ceiling and continued on until eventually breaking through the desert ground and soaring into the sky above.

Impressed, Hopkins stepped forward into the ray of light beaming down from the ceiling and stared up through the hole Adam had just created. "Wow. I really didn't know he could do that."

Distraught by the turn events, Sarah backed herself against the wall and fell to the floor in shock. "He...he's gone."

Christine walked over to kneel down beside her as Jason approached Hopkins. "I think it's safe to say Adam's officially AWOL. I'll organize the search."

"That won't be necessary," said Hopkins, shaking his head. "Tyran's priority number one."

Jason was puzzled but also aggravated by the directive. "Forget Tyran. Adam could be going anywhere. We need to find him."

Again, Hopkins brushed off the idea by shaking his head. "It doesn't matter. We won't get to him in time."

Confused by the comment, Christine stood while helping Sarah off the floor. "In time for what?"

Hopkins turned towards the doorway. "Tell them doctor."

They all looked over to find Dr. Groves entering the room. "As unfortunate as it may be, the boy will die in the next couple of days."

"What are you talking about?" asked Christine.

The doctor stopped just inside the doorway and stood with his hands clasped behind his back. "When we performed the super soldier procedure on Adam I had his body hooked on a dependency drug."

Jason walked up to enter the doctor's personal space. "A what?"

"A dependency drug," answered Groves, staring Jason down. "It does exactly what it sounds like. The chemical makes a subject's body dependent on it. It doesn't affect a person physically or mentally, but their body needs it to survive. I've been giving Adam injections of it every morning since the procedure. Without it, he'll be dead before we have a chance to find him."

Furious with the news, Jason grabbed the doctor by his lab coat and pressed him against the wall. "You think he's just a lab rat you can do whatever you want with?! What's the matter with you?!"

Clearly not in any rush to intervene, Hopkins slowly walked over to them. "It was my idea. I told him to do it. The drug was a failsafe incase the boy ever got smart with his new powers and decided to leave, which I guess he finally did."

Christine reared her hand back ready to slap him across the face, but refrained from thrusting her arm forward, clenching her first instead. "What's wrong with you? He's just a boy."

Quite pleased with himself, Hopkins looked down at her with a devious grin. "That 'boy' is a weapon. Nothing more. Nothing less. But a weapon you can't control is useless. Adam should've known that he never owned that power inside him. His body and the abilities it possesses are my property to be used as I see fit. If he couldn't understand that...then he dies."

The rest of the room was speechless, unable to formulate a response. They just stared at Hopkins, all except Wolf, who walked past them as she stumbled towards the door. "I...I need air."

Hesitant to let her go, Christine and Jason looked at Hopkins once last time and shook their heads in disgust before following Wolf out of the room.

# 33

A dam didn't plan to fly anywhere fast. He just planned to fly. For a full day the boy enjoyed the desert's solitude, periodically soaring over forests and sporadic pockets of civilization. Every mile of his journey west seemed better than the last. The air was crisp and the silence was tranquil. Eventually, the land far below Adam came to end even though the sky did not. He considered continuing on, allowing the clouds to guide him forward.

But that was not the fate he chose.

Adam stopped at the edge of a rocky cliff overlooking the water and contemplated sitting there forever, just allowing the blazing sun to burn away the past seventeen years of his life. Although different than the ocean he grew up with in New York, California's coast was just as impressive and more beautiful in its own right. It would've served as a serene final image if he were to choose to close his eyes, never to open them again.

He distinctly remembered that being the exact moment he felt the pain.

At first he thought it was just hunger, but no food could make the pounding in his chest go away. Then came the fever, followed by sweats and chills. For days Adam wandered Los Angeles in a delirium, unable to relieve himself of the crippling agony growing inside of him.

By nightfall of the third day, the suffering had become too great to bear. Fully aware of his impending doom, Adam turned from a crowded street into a desolate alley, away from curious eyes. He limped a few steps through the pouring rain before stumbling against a dumpster from a coughing fit. With each dry heave growing more intense, Adam eventually coughed out a spray of blood across the side of a brick wall. He then grabbed onto his chest, letting out several grunts of pain before falling into a pile of garbage behind him.

Looking up into the sky with heavy, bloodshot eyes, Adam thought of many things, none of which were very funny. But he laughed anyway. "Here I come, Travis. Guess I wasn't so special after all."

Tired, hungry, and covered in wet clothes, the boy's chilled body shivered uncontrollably as he closed his eyes, ready to accept his fate.

"I hope you're not giving up yet," said an oddly familiar voice from deeper in the alleyway.

Adam struggled to look up but he did, just in time to see the old woman covered in rags and dirt emerge from the shadows. He tried to stand but could only squint as he curiously stared forward, barely able to recognize the face through the air. "Hey. I know you."

"Yes, Adam," she said with a nod, stopping about half way to him. "You do know me. It's been a long time, hasn't it?"

He summed up the strength to roll off the pile of garbage and sit up on his knees in the filth of the alley ground. "You saved me in New York."

The hideous woman nodded again while walking over to the boy and crouching down beside him. "You need to stop getting yourself into trouble. I might not be there to help you next time."

The woman gently placed her hands on Adam's chest and a white, glowing light radiated out from her palms. Adam could feel the pain leave his body in an instant and looked up at the woman with shocked, exhausted eyes of gratitude. "How...how did you do that?"

She reciprocated his look of disbelief with a smile. "It seems that some people didn't want you alive in the outside world."

"Who are you?" asked Adam, still in shock of her healing abilities.

Ignoring the question, the woman simply caressed the side of his cheek with her wrinkly, wart-covered hand. "You have a lot of work to do, Adam. Get some rest. Your day shall come."

Satisfied with a job well done, the woman stood and walked deeper into the alley when Adam called out to her. "Tell me. I need to know. Why are you helping me?"

She never turned around but answered his question as she returned to the darkness. "We all have a purpose, Adam. Even gods."

# PART III
## PROVIDENCE

"Death solves all problems."

Joseph Stalin – Dictator

# 34

Life had been relatively calm for Adam after escaping The Armory, yet that didn't mean he wasn't busy. It was hard to tell because he couldn't step outside his own skin, but Adam assumed the past three years of freedom had a noticeable effect on him. His body had matured. Now in his twenties, Adam was taller than before and his face had roughed out by shedding its boyish façade. He'd grown more perceptive, as well, and stood with a comfortable confidence only a worldly experience could bestow. It was a poise he sorely lacked during his time as a child soldier, super powers or not.

But the time for self-discovery had passed. While his three-year vision quest wasn't without purpose, Adam was ready for what came next and found himself in the Florida panhandle to accomplish it.

He wore a rather unimposing white t-shirt and ripped jeans along with a worn set of sneakers that seemed ten years past their expiration date. The sky was bright and the trailer park he strolled through was filled with people joyously taking advantage of the Florida sun. Most of them were families, parents and children shooting squirt guns or playing catch. But this small town, the name of which Adam hadn't even bothered to learn, wasn't without its decadent class.

Adam spotted such an individual aimlessly wandering by the park's entrance as a car pulled up to the curb beside him.

Wearing nothing but a thin undershirt and baggy shorts, the scrawny man leaned into the car and casually shook hands with the driver, a sloppy and indiscreet transfer of goods. After the exchange was complete, the man left the entrance to head back into the trailer park when Adam purposefully took a route to cross paths with him. "Yo. What's up?" From this close, Adam finally noticed the bright red sunburns covering the man's arms and neck.

Aggravated to have someone in his path, the man kept his hand over a bulge in his waistline as he looked Adam up and down. "I know you?"

"I need to buy," Adam stated dryly, refusing to look anywhere other than the man's eyes.

The man laughed and made a move to pass around Adam. "I don't know what you're talking about, kid. Get on outta here."

Leaning into his path, Adam waved a rolled up wad of money in the man's face, which stopped him in his tracks. "I brought cash. A friend told me where to find you."

The man looked Adam up and down again, curious yet suspicious at the same time. "You five-O or somethin'?"

"Nah, man," Adam said with a playful smirk. "Do I look like a cop? I'm just looking to get hooked up like everyone else."

The man vigilantly scanned around them for prying eyes before subtly waving Adam to follow him. "Aight. Come on."

He brought Adam to a small, rundown trailer in the corner of the park. Unsurprisingly, the inside of the doublewide looked much the same way as it did on the outside. Moldy carpeting was half pulled up and covered in empty Chinese food boxes. Beer bottles, some still half full, were scattered around the living room in between cigarette packed ashtrays and pornographic magazines.

As he waited in front of an uncovered mattress that served as the couch, Adam surveyed the trailer's smoke stained ceiling. "This is a nice place you got here."

The man walked up from the back bedroom, holding a Ziploc bag of white powder in his hand. "Not really. How much you want?"

Adam leaned forward to stare at it and nodded. "The whole bag."

Abruptly pulling his arm back, the man reached into his shorts, pulled out the Glock 19 that was tucked inside, and held it sideways as he nonchalantly pointed it at Adam. "Actually, I changed my mind. Gimme the money, bitch."

In the blink of an eye, Adam stepped up to the side, grabbed the man's wrist, and then shoved the heel of his other hand through the dealer's forearm. The force of Adam's strike broke the man's radius in two, causing the man to scream in unbelievable pain.

Unmoved by the man's agony, Adam held up what was left of the hand still clutching the pistol. "You shouldn't play with guns. Might hurt yourself."

The man dropped to the floor screaming while blood spurt wildly around the living room from the stump of his arm. He began flailing uncontrollably on the floor as Adam casually removed the gun from the severed hand. After placing his foot on the man's chest to pin him down, the super soldier then tossed the useless body part over his shoulder and shoved the gun's barrel straight through the man's forehead. "Like that."

The man instantly went motionless with the weapon imbedded deep into his caved-in skull. Adam stepped over the body to pick the bag of white powder off the floor and then sat down on the mattress. He proceeded to break the substance up into several smaller bags on the table, all while ignoring the growing pool of blood in the living room. Once he had enough, Adam placed the smaller bags into his pocket and put on an outfit similar to what the man was wearing from clothes laying around the room.

Looking the part of a drug dealer, Adam left the trailer to return to the park entrance. He strutted back and forth, imitating the scrawny man's swagger as best he could. It didn't take long for a car parked on the road opposite the trailer park to call him over. "Kid! Over here!"

Adam jogged over to the beat up, old station wagon and leaned into the passenger side window. "Don't call me kid. What you want?"

"My bad," said the middle aged black man inside. "I just noticed you walking out of Hunter's place. You his new boy?"

Pretending to be interested in the man's proposal, Adam lifted his chin to look deeper into the car. "Depends. How much you got?"

The man held up a thin strip of tightly folded bills. "Forty bucks."

Adam nodded with a smile as he reached into his pocket and grabbed one of the small bags inside. "For forty I might be."

He then reached into the car and slapped the man's hand, subtly exchanging the two items in the process. "Enjoy."

Adam only made it halfway back to the trailer park entrance before he heard the sirens. The crowd gathered around the street instantly scattered as cop cars with flashing lights swarmed around Adam in a manner of seconds. A moment later and the men driving the cars all stepped out with their guns drawn. Adam started to lift his arms in the air when a hand suddenly grabbed the back of his head and tripped him down, slamming his face hard into the pavement.

The next thing Adam felt was a firm knee dug into his back as his wrists were pulled around and placed in cuffs. "You are under arrest for the distribution of illegal narcotics. Anything you say can and will…"

Adam had already toned out the words, focusing instead on two grabby hands feeling around his pockets and pulling out a handful of small baggies. He was then lifted off the street and shoved into the back of the only unmarked cop car surrounding them. After falling back onto the seat, Adam ran his fingers over the cold metal of the handcuffs locked behind his back and stared up at the car's ceiling with a smile.

# 35

Although a lot had changed for Wolf in the three years since Adam left her life, where she slept, however, had not. She still laid her head in the same bed her and Adam once shared. But after years of practice, the soldier had learned to push thoughts of that night far from her mind.

For some people, that had to change.

Emerging from the darkness inside the room, the old woman who had helped Adam survive his escape from The Armory walked over to Wolf, who slept peacefully in her bed. The woman then took a soft breath, gently placing her wrinkled hand over Wolf's head. "Dream of your love, pretty girl."

Wolf's eyes fluttered in her sleep as images of Adam standing atop a fiery volcano entered her mind. Staring down at a deep, treacherous pit of lava, the super soldier looked older than the boy she remembered. He leaned forward just enough to fall off the edge. Plummeting downward, Adam picked up speed in his descent before plunging head first into the bubbling pit of molten rock.

Wolf woke from her dream in a sweaty panic, rapidly gasping for air. As she calmed herself, the young woman couldn't shake the feeling that she wasn't alone yet was surrounded by nothing but darkness.

Wolf stood and walked to the small bathroom attached to the room and ran the faucet to splash water on her face. She then looked at her exhausted reflection in the mirror, which stared back at her with two eyes invigorated with life. "He's alive."

Wolf couldn't sleep for the rest of the night. At the break of dawn, she scoured the facility's halls for the one person she knew wouldn't call her crazy and quickly hurried through a crowd to catch up to her. "Christine, wait."

After letting out a half-annoyed sighed, Christine stopped in the middle of the hall and turned to Wolf. "I'm busy. What is it?"

"I need to speak with you."

"About?" asked Christine impatiently.

Wolf opened her mouth to speak but had to force the words to come out. "I...I think Adam's alive."

Christine rolled her eyes as she turned to walk away. "Adam's been dead for three years."

Quickly hopping forward, Wolf stepped in front of Christine, blocking her path. "I had this weird dream last night. Only it wasn't really a dream. More like a picture burned into my head."

After taking a deep, settling breath, Christine relaxed her tense demeanor and put a concerned hand on Wolf's shoulder. "It's probably stress. You've seen a lot of combat lately. Just get some rest and you'll be fine. "

Frustrated by her tone, Wolf pushed Christine's hand away and raised her voice. "He's alive!"

Sensing the attention they were getting from the curious crowd passing them by, Christine grabbed more firmly onto Wolf's arm and subtly pulled her to the side of the hall. "That's not something you want to yell around here."

Wolf ignored her concern though, focusing back to the topic at hand. "What I felt wasn't normal. Adam's alive. I know it."

Christine stood tall and crossed her arms with a grimace, a sign she was at least willing to entertain the idea. "Ok. Let's say you're right. He is alive. What are we going to do about it? Or more importantly, what *can* we do about it?"

"Find him," declared Wolf, her eyes firm with conviction. "We have to."

# 36

Several hours after his arrest, Adam sat beside a desk in the middle of a busy precinct floor. His wrists rested in his lap, bound together by handcuffs. Filled wall to wall with cluttered desks, the one-story police station buzzed with activity as federal officers navigated the chaos, many of whom had a wide assortment of colorful characters in custody. A loud flow of chatter bounced off the building's textured ceiling intermixed with the constant hum of ringing phones.

In front of Adam sat a large man in an undersized uniform completely focused on taking as big a bite from his overstuffed sandwich as possible. He then dropped his lunch on the desk and proceeded to talk to Adam with his mouth full of food.

Uninterested in what he had to say, Adam ignored the officer to examine his surroundings. In the corner of the room Adam spotted an old air conditioner boarded up in the window. The broken appliance explained the many small fans scattered throughout the precinct, all fighting to disperse the thick humidity festering in the air. Every window in the place was open, but battling the mugginess was futile given the commotion adding to the heat in the overcrowded room.

Continuing his observation along the same path, Adam began focusing on the water bottles and towels stacked along the wall when the talking officer finally nabbed his attention. "You hear me, kid? I'm trying to help you."

Adam turned to him with a contrite smile. "I'm sorry, officer."

"Whoa. An apology. Don't get many of those from your kind." The man's genuine surprise faded as he began flipping through one of the many folders strewn across his desk. "So, you're facing possession and distribution charges but lack any form of identification. You got a name you're willing to give me?"

"Adam."

Still scanning the folder's contents, the man's eyebrows rose as he nodded. "Ok. That's a start. You have a last name, Adam?"

Waiting for an answer, the man looked up to find Adam's empty eyes blankly staring back at him. The officer waited another moment before accepting Adam's silence as an answer and then returned his eyes to the folder in his hands. "Ok. Never mind then. Do you know where you live? Do you know where you're from?"

"New York," replied Adam, plainly.

The man again looked up from his folder. "You're a long way from home. Any idea why you're here?"

"I wanted to see, one last time, if the system is worth saving. If the fate I have chosen for our species is correct. Now I understand it has to be. Because all this is nothing but failure. Or more accurately...we've failed ourselves."

Shutting the folder in frustration, the man leaned over his desk to get closer to Adam. "What's your problem, kid?"

"I'm not the problem..."Adam slowly stood from his seat as tiny sparks began sporadically flickering around his body. "...I'm the solution."

In awe of the strange lights manifesting in front of him, the man stood from his desk, fearfully drawing his gun and aiming it in Adam's direction. "Ju—just sit down."

With his hands still lowered, Adam casually jerked his arms apart, ripping the metal restraints in two. The man's eyes shot open in disbelief and the room's commotion slowly withered into silence as everyone turned to the strange electricity growing around Adam's body.

"Sit down now or I will fire!" demanded the man, his legs now shaking in terror.

Refusing the order, Adam slowly raised his arm with a single finger pointed at the man's chest. "No. You won't."

Although backing away, the man pressed his gun forward

as if to intimidate his target. "Sit down, freak!"

The other officers drew their weapons and pointed them at Adam while everyone else in the room ducked behind the desks for cover. The flashes of bright blue electricity building around Adam's body slowly started to converge along his arm and into the tip of his extended finger. "Bang."

A thin line of energy shot out of Adam's finger like a laser and straight through the man's chest. The force of the blast sent the man's body soaring backwards and slamming into the far wall of the precinct. There was a moment of shocked hesitation in the room as the man fell to the floor and began convulsing uncontrollably from the visible surges of electricity running up and down his body.

Before the twitching corpse came to a stop, every officer in the room opened fire in Adam's direction. He didn't move though, allowing the electricity dancing around his body to strike down every bullet headed towards him. The slugs all fell to the floor, dented and charred, and Adam sprung into action as the frazzled officers frantically scrambled to reload their weapons.

Leaping from desk to desk, Adam kicked the officers in his path, sending their bodies flying across the room. He then flipped to the ground and punched an officer directly in front of him, plunging his fist straight through the man's chest. With the cop now dangled from his wrist, Adam flung his arm to the side and sent the body flying into a crowd of officers that had given up reloading their guns.

One after another, the officers charged at Adam with whatever weapons they were able to draw in the moment, but the batons and knives were no match for the super soldier. Adam killed them all, including whatever fearful pedestrians were attempting to flee through the front door or out the back of the building. He massacred everyone in sight, allowing their bodies to fall to the floor before stepping over them and continuing on in a calm rage. The slaughter only lasted a few minutes, but by the time it was over, Adam was the only human being left alive in the precinct.

# 37

L arge droplets of water, leftover from last night's rainfall, splashed off the jungle's thick leaves as Tyran barged into them. He was sprinting, his bare chest covered in muggy sweat and scratches from the dense brush in his way. He wore camouflaged pants and tight boots that stretched up to his shins, the only kind of clothing he felt comfortable in anymore. Thin rays of sunshine barely made it through the tall canopy above and down to the rainforest floor, lighting the way as Tyran ran through and around the branches in his path before ultimately stopping to catch his breath.

Leaning against the trunk of a large tree, Tyran's attention shot up when a harsh voice spoke to him from deep within the jungle. "All this training and you really think of yourself as a warrior?"

Tyran wandered forward into a clearing and spun around looking for the source of the voice as it continued to speak. "But I've observed Spartans raise their children with swords in their hands. I've watched Aztecs dance happily over the bodies of their enemies. And I've seen Mongols lay waste to entire cities just to watch them burn. They are true warriors. You are nothing."

After narrowing down where the taunts had come from, Tyran stared firmly in a singular direction. "Enough theatrics. Show yourself."

The plants and brush in front of him rustled as the old woman in rags emerged from behind them and stopped in the clearing. "I hope you haven't forgotten about me."

"No," said Tyran, stiffening his back upon looking at the

unsightly woman. "I haven't. Should I even wonder how you found me?"

The woman smirked. "Nothing is beyond my reach, Andrew. Nothing is above my influence."

Rolling his eyes at her continued dramatics, Tyran turned his back on the woman as he prepared to resume his run. "That's great. But I'm busy. Come back later."

He pushed on through the jungle only to take several steps and find the woman standing in front of him. "When I came to you in that prison we made a deal."

Shocked to see her, Tyran looked the frail, unimposing woman up and down. "How did you—"

"It's time for you to hold up your end," she stated, cutting of his puzzlement.

Wiping the surprise from his face, Tyran stood tall and took a deep, sobering breath. "It's been three years. What took the boy so long?"

"Adam needed time to understand his role. He's growing stronger than I expected, though, and I feel his intentions have gone in a different direction from what I hoped."

"What do you need me for?" Tyran asked, respectfully.

"Isn't it obvious?" The woman tilted her head to the side with a smile. "I need you to set him straight."

Very little had changed in Hopkins's isolated office since he first moved in after The Armory was built. The furniture, carpeting, even the light bulbs remained untouched. The most recent addition, though, was not actually located in the office but a secretary just outside the door. Hopkins was quickly discovering, though, that having an assistant was often more trouble that it was worth.

He sat quietly behind his desk looking over an analysis report when the intercom on his phone suddenly clicked. "Mr. Hopkins, I'm sorry to interrupt you, but…"

The secretary's voice trailed off, hoping to be reprieved of any wrongdoing, but Hopkins was still unhappy as he leaned forward to speak into the desktop phone. "You're not sorry, otherwise you wouldn't be doing it. So when I say, 'don't interrupt me,' I mean, 'don't interrupt me.' "

"But there's something on the news you might want to see, sir," said the secretary, her voice anxiously quivering.

Deeply annoyed, Hopkins closed his eyes while rubbing his forehead. "What is it?"

There was a momentary pause on the other end of the line before the secretary spoke again. "I think you should come look for yourself."

Aggravated by the blatant disrespect, Hopkins practically pushed himself off of the desk and stormed out of the office door. "What is so damn—"

Once in the foyer, his eyes immediately hooked onto the television opposite the secretary's perpendicular desk. The snapshots on the screen, of what could only be described as a massacre, were hard to look away from. Even with the pixelated distortions covering the majority of the images, it was quite easy for the imagination to fill in the blanks of mutilated corpses and body parts littering the police precinct floor. Overturned desks, tables, and chairs, all covered in blood and gore, were thrown about the room as if a tornado ran through the building.

The carnage pretty much described itself, but the voice of a female reporter spoke over top of it anyway. "For those of you just tuning in, what you're looking at now is a police station in northern Florida. At least fifty people are dead in what appears to be one of the most brutal and horrific massacres in American history."

Although appalled, Hopkins hid his revulsion behind annoyance as he turned toward his secretary. "And why is this so important that I need to see it?"

"Keep watching," she replied, still seated behind her desk.

Rolling his eyes, Hopkins turned his attention back to the television as the reporter continued her broadcast. "The most mysterious part of this already bizarre crime is a message presumably left behind by the murderer. The words 'Hopkins, this is only the beginning' are smeared in blood along the wall. The police have not issued an official statement as to who this 'Hopkins' might be and if more killings are likely to take place. There's been no word on a suspect or motive behind these gruesome murders nor were there any survivors left behind at the scene."

Fighting his urge to stare at the television in shock, Hopkins once again turned to his secretary and frantically pointed towards the screen. "What channel is this on?"

Flustered by his sudden question, the startled secretary's eyes grew wide. "Uh…"

"What channel?!" Hopkins shouted.

She swallowed quickly to stammer out a response. "All of them. The Federal Information Station. American Credibility Front. US News Network…"

The secretary continued to talk, but Hopkins heard enough. He marched back into his office, slammed the door hard behind him and proceeded to pace nervously around the room. "Damn. This is not good. Not good at all."

A moment later, the phone on his desk rang and Hopkins stopped pacing to stare at it. He did nothing for several seconds but watch the flashing light on the phone's screen as it flickered.

Hopkins then anxiously wiped the budding sweat from his forehead and answered the call. "Hello. No, sir. I have no idea. It can't be him. Impossible. I'm terribly sorry. Yes. I know the consequences. I will handle it personally. You and the other partners have my word."

Hopkins hung up and sulked his head into his chest. He then took a deep breath to calm his nerves and reached back to the phone to contact his secretary. "I want Jason and Christine in the briefing room in ten minutes."

# 38

Scientists were easy to come by in Russia. The Soviet mind was particularly prone to critical thinking and testing ethical boundries. Mouths willing to keep a secret, however, were far harder to find.

Tyran soon discovered that it was the young ones fresh out university that were easily cajoled into silence. More importantly, they were apt to working long hours for little pay in the middle of a jungle. Such naiveté had yet to be corrupted by the world and was still eager for greatness, but after three years of failure, even the most ambitious individual could start to lose their patience.

Tyran was well aware of that as he entered the laboratory and found Molotok's head scientist, a thirty-three year old man with slicked back hair, standing over a counter.

"Good afternoon," said Tyran as soft and unimposing as possible.

Focused on reading his notes, the scientist never looked up as he greeted his guest in a thick Russian accent. "What do you want?"

Tyran stopped five feet from the man and spoke to his hunched over back. "Just to see if there's any progress."

Irritated by Tyran's presence, the scientist scoffed while keeping his head buried in his work. "What do you think? Three years and not a single successful subject. You brought me false information."

"I brought you everything they had," Tyran replied, his voice still low and humble.

The man shook his head, still having yet to look his visitor in the face. "Then you missed something."

Tyran burst forward, spinning the scientist around and grabbing him by the throat. He then pressed him forward over the countertop, crushing the scientist's back against the glass equipment on the shelves above. "I told you, 'I brought you everything they had.' If you can't figure it out then it has nothing to do with the data."

Clawing at Tyran's grip around his neck, the man gasped out every word to speak. "But...but it should be working. You told me they ran a successful test. Why haven't we?"

Still pinning the man against the shelves, Tyran's focus moved down to the counter, where he picked up and examined several pages of hand scribbled notes. "Maybe it's not the test that's the problem. Maybe it's your subjects."

"What do you mean?" the man struggled to ask.

Tyran carelessly tossed the papers over his shoulder and returned his focus to the scientist. "Use me next."

Although struggling to breathe, the man still managed a confused expression. "Excuse me?"

Tyran eased his grip and lowered the man back down to the floor. "You're going to use me as your next test subject."

"I will not," said the man, regaining his dignity by adjusting his crumpled lab coat. "No more procedures until we get it right."

"If it weren't for me you vodka-loving bastards would have nothing."

The scientist nodded his head while swallowing deeply, trying to summon the courage to resist his attacker's demands. "That might be true but you're not of Russian blood. Molotok high command would never approve of it."

Tyran reached behind his back and removed a Makarov pistol, casually placing it against the scientist's head. "Who's going to tell them? Look at it this way: you don't do it and I kill you. But if you do it, and it succeeds, you're a genius. Or I die, in which case you'll never have to deal with me again. It's really a win-win situation for you."

Glancing back and forth between Tyran and the gun pressed against his temple, the cowering scientist closed his eyes and rapidly nodded his head. "Ok. I'll do it. Just…don't hurt me."

"Good," said Tyran, lowering the gun down to his side.

He then began wandering further down the counter, his eyes scanning the many project documents covered in broken glass as the scientist spoke. "But tell me: why do you think the procedure will work now if so many have died before you?"

Brushing several shards of glass aside, Tyran reached down and lifted a black and white photo of Adam from the counter. "Faith."

# 39

With Adam missing and presumed dead, Jason and Christine had to find new roles at The Armory. It wasn't difficult. As analysts by trade, there was plenty of data from the other projects to be scrutinized, but that didn't mean the super soldier they once looked after was ever far from their thoughts.

However, as they patiently sat in the squad's briefing room, they were confused by the question Hopkins posed as he barged through the door. "Is it him?"

Jason leaned forward, as if getting closer would help clarify his confusion. "Is it who?"

"The boy," said Hopkins, stopping in the center of the room. "Is he still alive?"

Even without mentioning him by name, there was only one person who Hopkins could be referring, so Jason leaned back, now disinterested in the topic. "It's been three years. You would know better than us."

Unhappy with the response, Hopkins pointed an angry finger that shifted back and forth between the two people seated in front of him. "Don't put this on me. He was your charge."

Christine didn't move except to shake her head in defiance. "We haven't been in contact with him if that's what you're asking."

Allowing his anxiety to take control, Hopkins began nervously pacing around the room. "Well, he's out there, and bringing him in should be our top priority. I want you looking into all of his—"

Jason stood, abruptly cutting him off. "This has nothing to do with us. Adam is dead. You made sure of that. So just leave me and Christine out it."

"It was him," declared a voice from the doorway.

The three of them turned to find Wolf standing tall with her hands clasped behind her back. "Adam's alive and he wants us to know it."

Hopkins grimaced as he casually waved the girl away. "This conversation is private."

"Tell them, Hopkins," demanded Wolf, ignoring his dismissal.

Curiously concerned, Christine stood from her seat, as well. "Tell us what?"

Hopkins wouldn't answer. He simply stared at Wolf, puzzled by her awareness. When Jason and Christine couldn't get a response from him they turned to Wolf. She didn't look back at them, continuing to coldly stare at Hopkins.

The standoff lasted for several seconds until Hopkins gave in and smirked, unashamed and unapologetic of his confession. "The super soldier program has been rebooted."

"What?" asked Jason, in disbelief of the news.

With the secret out, Hopkins relaxed his stance as he walked over to one of the chairs and slumped into it. "Molotok has begun running human tests for their own project. Luckily for us, they haven't succeeded, but we're not taking any chances. We started our own program back up in another secure facility. Clandestinely, of course."

Angered by the news, Christine stomped over to Hopkins's chair and stood over him. "You've been creating super soldiers this whole time?"

"Not really," said Hopkins, indifferently shaking his head. "After Groves's death we attempted to piece together what we had left of his notes but nothing worked. Every test resulted in the subject's death. To this day we still don't know why the procedure worked on Adam and no one else. He was...or I should say is...the only super soldier ever."

Wolf fully entered the room to stand beside Jason and Christine leering over Hopkins. "And now he wants a little payback for being your guinea pig."

Dispirited by the situation, Hopkins's gaze remained fixated on the floor. "I don't know how he survived."

"But he did," stated Wolf, her condemnation implied.

Snapping back into the seriousness of their situation, Hopkins sprang from his seat and resumed his march around the room. "Enough of this. Adam's alive and we need to find him. Any idea what this message means?"

"It wasn't addressed to us," said Christine, crossing her arms. "Why don't you figure it out?"

Jason firmly pressed his hands to his face as if to wipe away the stress. He then stated the first real helpful clue any of them had. "Adam's from New York. Maybe he's there."

Satisfied by the idea, Hopkins started towards the door. "Good. You and Christine go to the city and see if you can locate him. Wolf, have your team on site and ready to take him out."

"What?!" yelled Christine, angrily taking a single step forward. "Adam's not our responsibility anymore! Why do we have to go?"

Hopkins stopped in the doorway, his body half turned to answer the question. "You're the only two people he won't kill the first chance he gets. At least, I hope not."

He then left the room entirely and Christine humbly looked to Wolf. "I guess you were right."

"Unfortunately," said Wolf, starting to move towards the door.

She only managed two steps, though, when Jason reached out to stop her. "You don't have to do this if you don't want to. I know you have feelings for him."

"Had feelings," corrected Wolf. "Three years is a long time. I'm a soldier now and I have a job to do."

# 40

Even after travelling the world several times over, Adam concluded there was no place quite like Manhattan. It wasn't the towering skyscrapers or throngs of people packed into every square inch of land. It was the energy. There was something about the island itself that polarized everything about a person. The city could bring out the worst in someone just as easily as the best. It was a phenomenon Adam had both the pleasure and horror of experiencing firsthand.

He noticed not much had changed in his old uptown neighborhood since he left all those years ago. Federal policemen still wandered the streets, only performing a fraction of the job required of them. Even with depression crushing the community around him, Adam could stare straight up in wonder at the skyscrapers looming overhead. He imagined he looked like a midwestern tourist in awe of the Big Apple. In many ways he was, but Adam still felt more at home than he had in a long, long time.

He eventually came to a large intersection on the avenue across the street from a gas station-auto body shop on the corner. Two men in cheap seats with greasy hair sat outside the station's office and a sign that read "Trello's Garage" hung from a rusted chain above their heads. Briefly reading the name brought back images of Adam's dying father to his mind, but Adam pushed the horrifying memories aside as he took a deep breath and stepped forward to cross the intersection.

As he passed under the traffic light, an oncoming car slammed its brakes to keep from colliding with him. The driver then immediately honked her horn while sticking her head out the window. "Hey! Open your eyes, asshole!"

Adam ignored the infuriated woman and continued on a direct path towards the two men. Attracted by the commotion, both men instantly spotted Adam walking steadfast through the busy traffic, headed in their direction.

More curious than concerned, one of the two men leaned his head back and yelled into the open office doorway. "Uhh... Boss? There's some kid headed our way."

A man's grumbled voice yelled out from inside the station. "Take care of him."

"Like 'take care' of him?" asked the other man.

"Just deal with it, you idiot," the annoyed voice commanded.

The bigger of the two men stood from his chair and started walking forward to meet Adam in the middle of the gas station. Upon reaching the curb, Adam kicked up a serrated piece of scrap metal from the ground, catching it in mid-air and hurling it towards the man. The sharp metal shard flew like a dart straight into the man's neck, killing him instantly.

A fountain of blood sprayed in the air as the corpse dropped to the ground, and the other man, still seated by the office, fell backwards off his chair. "Holy shit!"

Scrambling to his feet, the man quickly fumbled for the pistol in its holster and opened fire in Adam's direction. Still marching forward, Adam sidestepped every bullet with ease as he fearlessly walked on and entered the center of the gas station.

Astonished, the man's eyes grew wide as he dropped the empty handgun to remove a folded switchblade from his pocket. "What the hell are you?"

He pressed a button, flipping up the knife within the blade's handle, and charged at Adam, wantonly swinging the weapon in a desperate plea to stab him. With his hands at his sides, Adam easily moved around the man's attacks before stepping aside and grabbing onto the man's arm. He then casually lifted the man straight up off the ground with one hand as Trello emerged from inside the office with a small mob of armed thugs. Raising their weapons, the men swarmed to cover every corner of the gas sation.

Once their intruder was surrounded, Trello himself casually

walked up to Adam, pointing a shotgun straight in his face. "Put him down. Now."

Adam released his grip on the man, dropping him to the ground. Trello then pulled the man back behind him without ever moving the shotgun away from Adam's head. "You must have some death wish, kid."

"That would imply you're actually capable of killing me," Adam replied, calm and expressionless.

Trello formed an ugly smirk in response. "You got balls. I'll give you that. But what could make you crazy enough to come after me unarmed in my own place?"

Adam answered the question without blinking. "You killed my father."

"I've killed a lot of fathers," said Trello, unimpressed.

"And none were probably more deserving than mine."

Confused by his attacker's relaxed demeanor, Trello looked at Adam sideways. "So what is this then? You came to thank me?"

"No. You don't deserve my gratitude," said Adam plainly, as if stating a fact. "What you deserve is to be the first to die."

Trello pumped the shotgun a single time, his face mean and cringed. "Sounds like you want a reunion with your old man."

Rather than attack though, Adam strangely knelt down to a small metal circle beneath his feet, an action that left Trello confused. "What the hell are you doing?"

Adam didn't respond. He simply raised his fist into the air and punched the metal disk, popping it out of the ground and high into the air.

Amazed by the feat, Trello slowly lowered his weapon in awe. "How did you do that?"

Ignoring the question, Adam stood and held out his palm turned up towards the sky. A small flame of blue energy formed in the center of his hand, and again, Trello stared at his mysterious visitor in perplexed wonder. "What the...?"

Suddenly pulling his arm back, Adam let the small flame fall from his hand and drop straight down. It was only then, as the flame plunged through the hole in the ground left by the missing metal cap, did Trello's look of amazement turn to horror. "Get down!"

Trello and his men all turned to sprint away from the station as a large chain of explosions erupted from underneath the pavement. The blast erupted upwards, engulfing the gas station office and pumps while tossing cars and Trello's men across the street.

A large, towering fireball tore up into the sky, sending a cloud of black smoke billowing over top the neighborhood. A thick wave of dust covered the entire street corner, and as it faded, small fires continued to blaze around the rubble and ruins of the devastated gas station

In the middle of the intersection, Trello had only just started to feel the agony of the burns wrapped around his shaking body. His ravaged hands were covered in blood and boils, his face mutilated with too many cuts and scratches to count. Still, with a rush of adrenaline surging through his veins, the mobster managed to slowly rise to his hands and knees.

Fighting the brutal pain screaming in his head, Trello looked up to see a small figure covered in flames before him. The flaming man emerged from the smoke wafting through the gas station wreckage and approached Trello in the intersection. With every step forward, Trello could feel the inferno's heat more and more. Soon, the fire surrounding the man started to simmer down, revealing Adam beneath the flames. He was naked except for the ash and smoldering cinder smeared over his perfectly unharmed body.

Terrified beyond belief, Trello attempted to stand only to fall backwards and begin desperately crawling away. "I…I'm sorry. Please…mercy…I beg you."

Stopping over Trello's mangled form, Adam extended a fiery hand, allowing the energy to build in his palm. "This is mercy."

"No!" screamed Trello, his voice throaty and weak.

He then lifted his arms to shield himself from the blast as Adam unleashed a wave of concentrated flames that engulfed his entire body.

All around the decimated street corner, panicked witnesses sprinted away from the scene as curious onlookers approached for a closer look. As they arrived, Adam had already vanished down an alleyway, where he found a spare set of clothes to throw over his body. They were filthy, pulled from a garbage can that hadn't been dumped in days, but Adam didn't mind. Truthfully, he never felt cleaner in his life.

# 41

Jason and Christine had very little motivation to visit New York and search for Adam. While they might've certainly cared for him as a boy, he just wasn't that person anymore. After Groves's procedure turned Adam into a living weapon, the analysts tried to remain as close to him as they once were, but it was difficult forming a relationship with a teenage boy under normal circumstances, let alone one trained to be a child soldier with super powers.

Jason and Christine had worked hard over the past three years to keep Adam from their thoughts. Going on a manhunt for him in a city of eight million people was hardly what they were hoping for. Even more than that, though, the two of them had no idea where to begin. They tried scoping out places that had been important to him. His childhood apartment, St. Maria's, even the alley where his father was murdered. But they couldn't find a clue of Adam's whereabouts let alone a sign that he had been there recently.

Jason had simply resorted to driving in circles around Adam's old neighborhood, hoping to get lucky or hit a spark of inspiration. Christine sat quietly in the passenger seat, her face nearly pressing against the window.

Suddenly, a loud boom violently shook the street and the car along with it, forcing Jason to slam on his brakes. "Did you feel that?"

Christine sat up in her seat, looking around at the traffic jam surrounding them. "You think it was Adam?"

"Possibly," answered Jason, indifferent to the development.

Christine, however, had a tone more cautiously optimistic

than her partner. "Should we check it out?"

Jason shrugged his shoulders. "Not like we have anything better planned."

He maneuvered the car to turn around in the gridlock and drove in the opposite direction towards a cacophony of police and ambulance sirens. They only managed to get three blocks before Christine excitedly leaned forward to point out the windshield. "There! Right there! It's him."

Jason glanced across the street to spot a young homeless man, filthily dressed in a tattered outfit, walking towards them. His face looked as Adam would've if he were three years older than the last time they saw him, but Jason still wasn't convinced. "Are you sure?"

"Yes," answered Christine with the utmost confidence. "He's dressed like a bum but that's Adam. I'm sure of it."

That was all Jason needed to hear as he inconspicuously turned into and then back out of a parking garage. "All right. Let's see where he's going."

Carefully keeping their distance, the car followed Adam up and over several blocks to an old train car diner lodged between two monstrous brick buildings. After parking across the street, the partners sat in silence, eyeing the building for a full minute before Jason finally turned off the car. "I say we go in."

"What?" asked Christine, looking to him as if he had lost his mind.

Jason was absolutely serious, though. "Don't you want to see him?"

Christine grimaced as she reluctantly shrugged her shoulders. "Well...kind of. But it's been three years. He isn't the same Adam we knew. Do you really want to go in there and face that?"

Contemplating a decision, Jason looked at the diner for a moment before turning back to Christine. "I do."

"Fine," she said, hesitantly reaching for the door handle. "But we're getting out of there the first bad vibe I get."

Jason opened his door, as well. "Agreed."

Together, the two of them walked side by side to cross the street and enter the busy diner. Pushing their way through a crowd at the entrance, Jason and Christine both spotted Adam at the same time in a back booth by himself. They slowly walked over to the table and Adam addressed them without looking away from the burger in his hands. "I was wondering when you two would get out of the car."

Jason stepped up beside the table, keeping Christine behind him. "You knew we were here?"

Adam took a big bite of his food before answering with his mouth full. "Come on, Jason. You know me better than that. I can smell your cheap cologne from a mile away. Please, have a seat."

Jason and Christine cautiously moved over to the empty seat and slide into the booth. They then waited patiently as Adam chewed and swallowed before speaking again. "I'm guessing Hopkins sent you to find me. Am I right?"

"Like you always are," said Jason nodding.

Unconcerned with manners, Adam grabbed a handful of fries from the plate in front of him and shoved them in his mouth. "Did they start the super soldier project back up again?"

Again, Jason nodded. "How'd you know?"

Adam swallowed and reached for the glass of soda next. "Hopkins is too power hungry not to."

"He said he only did it in response to Molotok starting their own."

"And around and around we go." Adam rolled his eyes sarcastically. "And let me guess: neither has had a successful procedure?"

Now appearing surprised, Jason nodded for the third time. "You know everything don't you?"

Adam shook his head as he sipped from the soda's straw. "Not as much as I'd like to. How is Groves handling being Hopkins's tool again?"

"I don't think he cares that much since he died two years ago in a laboratory explosion," Jason said with a regretful grimace.

Indifferent to the news, Adam placed the glass back down on the table. "That's too bad."

The conversation lulled for a moment and Adam lifted his burger back off the plate. As he did, Christine stared into his eyes, attempting to read them before changing the subject.

"What have you been up to, Adam?"

"Oh, just some traveling." He took another bite of his burger and went on while chewing. "Someone once told me that's what young people my age are supposed to be doing and, you know, not locked in an underground facility training to kill people."

Ignoring his sarcasm, Christine showed genuine interest in Adam's story. "How was it?"

Still holding the burger in one hand, he used the other to wipe a drop of ketchup from his lip with a napkin. "You want to hear something interesting? I've been to every corner of the globe and seen more in three years than most do in a lifetime. Yet my absolute favorite places to hang out are diners like this one. I mean, just look around you. Everybody loves diners. It doesn't matter who you are. People of all walks of life come through that door and eat under the same roof simply because they're hungry. It's truly humanity at its finest."

Jason exchanged another slight glance with Christine before broaching a more sensitive subject with the super soldier. "A lot of people are mad at you, Adam, for what you did in Florida."

"I know," stated Adam while taking another bite.

Shocked by his callous response, Christine's back stiffened in her seat. "You don't have anything to say for yourself?"

Slightly perturbed by her condescending tone, Adam finished chewing and placed the burger down on his plate. "You wouldn't...you couldn't understand. I—"

Christine leaned forward over the table, cutting him off. "They were innocent people, Adam, and you slaughtered them for no reason at all. Do you even care—?"

Adam abruptly slammed his hand down on the flimsy table, rattling the glass, plates, and silverware on top of it. "Do I care? Do I care?! I'm the only one who does care!"

Jason looked around at the curious eyes starting to turn in their direction. "Adam, calm down. Just try to explain it. Tell us what you mean."

Adam took a deep breath to calm his nerves and then spoke with a more restrained ferocity. "Three years. For three years I walked around like a god among men. Do you know what that power is like? Do you have any idea? I could do whatever

I wanted at any moment I wanted and no one could stop me."

Still leaning across the table, Christine shook her head. "That doesn't make what you did right."

Adam leaned forward as well, looking right into her eyes with a frustrated smirk. "Open your eyes, Christine. Can't you see the amount of people that are hungry, suffering, and in pain around the world? The amount of people that are dying from disease and war every day? And here I am, the pinnacle of human achievement, and yet completely unable to stop any of it. Now you tell me if that's right?"

Christine wanted to say something but she didn't have an answer. Her rigid face softened and Adam saw it as an opening to monologue. "We humans are greedy and selfish yet driven by guilt and righteousness. The very nature of our existence is a contradiction. We strive for a utopia on this planet we'll never reach. A civilization that has treated its people this horribly does not deserve to exist."

This time Christine put the pieces together in her head before opening her mouth to speak. "So what are you saying, Adam? You're going to destroy humanity?"

Adam picked up whatever was left of his burger and shoved the whole thing into his mouth. "No. First I'm going to finish eating."

Jason took a deep breath and reluctantly asked a question to which he was afraid to know the answer. "Then what?"

"Then I'm going to systematically wipe out every city on the globe. One by one."

Jason's jaw hung open as he watched Adam casually wash down his food with the soda. He then realized it wasn't a joke. "You're serious, aren't you?"

"Deathly." Adam stared Jason down until realizing it was a poor word choice. "No pun intended."

Christine uncomfortably writhed in her seat with a look of concerned confusion. "Adam, I remember what you were like when you came back from Afghanistan. After Hopkins made you butcher all those people. It horrified you to be his killing machine. Is that really who you want to be?"

Adam shrugged his shoulders, apathetic and heartbroken.

"That's what they made me for, Christine. Not for love and compassion. But for war and chaos. So what else would you have me do? I can draw unlimited power at my fingertips yet I'm powerless to help anyone in any real way that matters. My body is nothing more than a tool of destruction and murder. But I've embraced it. I understand what I'm supposed to do. This is how I save a species unable to save itself."

Christine shook her head, dropping it into her chest. "I used to feel for you, Adam. I used to sympathize with what they put you through. But now...you've lost it. This is insanity. All that power has finally gone to your head."

Adam looked at her with heavy eyes and a bittersweet smile. "No, my dear Christine. This power was a gift and it changed me. If only you could see the world...see humanity through my eyes. Every living thing dies yet humans are the only species on this planet that fear death so much that they will do anything to stay alive. Why? Death is inevitable. People shouldn't fear it. They should accept it. Only then can this planet know peace."

After surveying the blank expressions on their faces, Adam turned to look out at the diner's happy patrons, oblivious of the super soldier seated amongst them. "Our pride and ego as a species has become too great. We've become too smart and too powerful for our own good. We create weapons to destroy yet say it's in the name of peace. We build glorious buildings and monuments that get knocked down and blown up simply because people have different opinions than one another."

He then turned his attention back to Jason and Christine seated across from him. "You might think of what I'm doing as destroying humanity, but I see it as saving it from an inevitable destiny of horror and torment."

Christine fought the urge to cry, but a single tear managed to slip out and slowly fall down her cheek. "You really don't believe that, Adam. You're sick. Come back with us. We can help you. This isn't you."

Adam shook his head with a regretful frown. "I'm sorry, Christine. I really am, but I need to do what I feel is right. Goodbye."

He then stood and carried his dirty plate to the counter

before exiting the diner.

# 42

Even though technically Manhattan's Harlem River Drive was prohibited for commercial vehicles, no one, not even the federal police, paid any attention to the white van speeding by as it weaved through traffic. Inside the van, eight soldiers, covered head to toe in modified versions of Molotok's commando armor, were seated on two benches mounted to the floor. Wolf, Toad, Tiger, and Colt, all waited quietly on one side while the squad's new, younger members sat opposite them. The women, Wasp and Viper, were positioned towards the front of the van while the men, Ram and Raptor, were closer to the back. The entire squad, veterans and recruits who had been working together for nearly a year, all sat peacefully with their backs against the van's walls, clutching a wide arsenal of weapons in their laps.

As the van swerved onto an avenue, Wolf looked up from staring at the floor to address the squad. "Some of you are personally acquainted with Adam Judson and some of you have only heard of him. Either way doesn't matter. Our mission is the same. He's a threat not only to this country but humanity as a whole. He is not to be left alive."

The newer members all looked around to gauge each other's reactions while those seated beside Wolf kept their gaze fixated as she went on. "Satellite photos show he's holed up in an abandoned apartment building. The area is heavily occupied with civilians. Normally I would advise discretion and stealth but Adam's trained as one of us. He knows our tactics, so we're to confront him head on."

Raptor lifted up the compact, lightweight grenade launcher

in his hands. "No kidding. I could take out a whole army with this thing let alone one man. I know he's a super soldier and all, but don't you think this is over doing it?"

After examining the green tipped ammunition loaded in her magazine, Viper nodded in agreement as she locked the clip into her modified M4 assault rifle. "Yeah. I don't know what they dipped these bullets in, but they're made from titanium. Isn't it a bit excessive to—"

Wolf leaned forward into the center of the van, cutting her off. "There is no such thing as excessive when it comes to Adam. He's not to be taken lightly. We need to hit him fast and with everything we have. These weapons are the only thing standing between you and certain death. You lose them and you're as good as a dead."

Viper gave a single curt nod and Wolf leaned back as Toad leaned over to her. "You sure about this, Wolf?"

She answered him with her eyes zoning out across the van, staring at nothing in particular. "I don't care if we have to take that whole building down with C4 and grenades. Adam needs to die. Does anyone object?"

Not even the recruits looked anywhere other than Wolf as she stood and grabbed onto the speeding van's ceiling. "Good. Let's go kill ourselves a super soldier."

The vehicle came to a rumbling stop and the back doors flung open. The eight soldiers, dressed in their heavily equipped combat gear, jumped out into the street and approached the five-story brick building in front of them. Ignoring the many astonished faces crowding the sidewalk, the squad fluidly flowed around the building's entrance and turned to Wolf for further instructions. "Once inside, we're splitting into two units. Viper, Ram, Toad, and Tiger will shoot up to the top floor and work their way down. The rest will come with me and we'll head up. Remember to radio in on the first sign of contact. Don't be a hero. It will take all of us to bring him down. So hold nothing back."

She gave a hand signal to Toad, who then cautiously turned the knob and pushed the door open. Viper and Ram slipped inside first with their weapons raised and ready to fire. After they cleared the small lobby area, Toad and Tiger came in next and directly approached the stairs with Viper and Ram falling in behind them. Together, the four soldiers watched each other's backs while tirelessly climbing the stairwell.

Once on the top floor, Toad stealthily led his team to the first apartment, where they broke off from the living area to check the bedrooms. Like the stairwell and lobby, the apartment was on the verge of being condemned. More paint chips covered the weathered wooden floors than the walls, and the only light let into the building came through thin slits on the boarded up windows.

Without any sign of Adam, Toad regrouped his unit and brought them to the apartment across the hall, which like the one before it, was also completely empty. He sent his three squad mates to search the area but again they returned with no news.

Frustrated by the lack of action, Toad lowered his weapon as he looked around and whispered. "It doesn't look like he's—"

Adam suddenly dropped down from the ceiling and landed behind him. He then stole the knife from Toad's belt and reached around to stab the soldier straight in the abdomen.

Screaming in pain, Toad's legs collapsed and he fell to the floor as Tiger lifted her weapon. "Toad!"

She fired a green stream of bullets, but Adam took off, running straight through the wall and into the first apartment they cleared.

Stepping up, Ram armed a grenade and tossed it through the open doorway. "Fire in the hole!"

Ram, Tiger, and Viper all dove to the ground as the explosion rocked the walls around them, blowing a hole out the side of the building and sending a rush of green flames through the hall.

With the dust settling, Tiger crawled over to Toad as he grunted painfully, drenched in blood. "Don't die, Toad. Hold on."

She then brought her arm up and began yelling into the communicator on her wrist. "Medic! We need a medic! Wasp, get up here and help—"

Adam cut Tiger off as he busted through the boarded

window in flight and tackled her straight into the wall. Tiger's body instantly went limp and dropped to the floor as Viper and Ram wasted no time opening fire from a knee. The bullets flashed as they left their rifles, but the super soldier moved around the room like a blur, dodging the green streaks by flipping through the air.

With an opening, Adam fired two quick blasts that knocked both soldiers to the ground and the guns from their hands. Ram and Viper then kicked up to their feet and charged ahead to engage Adam together. They let loose a synchronized series of kicks and punches, but the super soldier easily evaded every attempt to hit him. Spinning around, Adam finally ended the battle by kicking Ram through the door and then slipping behind Viper to snap her neck.

After clearing the apartments off of the lobby, Wolf and her team were already half way up the stairs to the second floor when the patter of gunfire echoed from above. "Get upstairs now!"

She led the way in a mad dash up the stairwell. As they passed the third floor a loud explosion shook the entire building and the group stopped to look around confused.

"Medic! We need a medic!" It was Tiger's desperate voice screaming at them through their wrist communicators. "Wasp, get up here and help—"

The rest of her message cut out and Wolf yelled her orders again. "Hurry! Move!"

They could hear the constant pop of gunfire all the way up the stairs, but by the time the unit reached the top floor there was only silence.

Wolf continued on ahead into the apartment where they found Toad on the floor with a knife in his stomach and Tiger lying limp in the corner with a giant splatter of her blood smeared against the wall. Ram and Viper were nowhere to be seen.

Scanning the room with her gun aimed ahead, Wolf quickly glanced in Wasp's direction. "Check them. Colt and Raptor, stay alert."

Wasp ran over to Tiger's body and checked her pulse before

moving over to Toad. "They're both dead."

The squad began wandering around the room and Raptor lowered his weapon in awe at the man-sized hole in the wall that looked as if someone ran through it. "What are we up against?"

Strolling past the window, Colt peeked outside through the broken boards to see the flashing lights of police cars along with a growing crowd of civilians on both sides of the street. "The cops are here."

Wolf responded while keeping her eyes vigilant and sharp. "Not our problem. Taking out the target is all that matters."

"Is that all I am to you, Sarah? A target?" said a familiar, haunting voice from behind her.

Wolf spun around but there was only an empty doorway. "You have no right saying my name."

She then backed herself deeper into the room while addressing her squad mates. "Shoot to kill. He could be anywhere."

Wasp stood from kneeling by Toad's body when Adam burst up through the floor, grabbed ahold of her, and continued flying upwards through the ceiling.

Startled, by the sudden abduction, Raptor swung his grenade launcher around in shock. "What was that?!"

Wolf lifted her hand to signal to the remaining members of her squad. "Tight formation."

Colt and Raptor closed in on Wolf and the three of them stepped into the hallway with their backs pressed together. Rotating in a circle, the three of them treaded carefully down the stairwell as Raptor nervously clenched onto the handle of his grenade launcher. "This is suicide. We lost the element of surprise. We can't take him like this."

Upon reaching the floor below, they moved into the hallway as a single, cohesive unit.

"No," said Wolf, responding to Raptor's fear with her eye locked through sight of her rifle. "We're not leaving until he's dead."

The voice returned, echoing through the walls. "Such harsh words. What happened to the Sarah I used to know? The Sarah I loved?"

Wolf continued looking ahead, carefully scanning to locate the voice's source. "You never loved me."

"I did," the voice replied softly. "And I know you felt the same way."

Wolf stopped in place, causing Raptor and Colt to do the same. She then smiled to herself while aiming at a nondescript spot in the wall. "Not anymore."

She fired a single shot with her M4 and the bullet pierced the wall as a scream came from the other side. Breaking their tight formation, Wolf kicked in the apartment's front door and discovered Adam in the living room, leaning against the wall and bleeding from his shoulder. "I see you have new toys."

"Just for you," she replied, her weapon trained directly at his head.

The other two soldiers followed her into the room and Colt smiled as he squeezed the trigger. "Too easy."

Diving over a hail of green gunfire from Colt's weapon, Adam sprung up and kicked Colt straight back into the wall. The injured super soldier then ran around the room as Wolf opened fire, her shots trailing just a split second behind his movements.

Aiming at a spot ahead on Adam's path, Raptor timed his shot and fired his launcher as Adam passed him by. The grenade round connected directly with the super soldier and exploded in a green burst, blasting him straight through the wall and down to the street below.

Impressed, Raptor held up the lightweight weapon with a smile on his face. "Damn. Can I use this thing all the time?"

Barely paying attention to the question, Wolf answered while helping Colt up to his feet. "Stay focused. We still have to finish the job."

Wolf and Colt wasted no time running out of the room, but Raptor trailed behind, confused by her comment. "Finish the job? But I just hit him with a grenade launcher."

# 43

Jennifer Thomspon had a gift for telling a story. At least, she thought she did. Which was why it was so frustrating for her to be stuck inside a local news van. Not that she thought there was anything wrong with reporting local news, especially in New York City, arguably the only place where local news mattered. But Jen always believed her gift for storytelling, not to mention her beautiful face, belonged on the federal networks.

As the van rocked back and forth through Manhattan's tight one-way streets, Jen swayed her compact mirror parallel to her body while skillfully applying her makeup.

Suddenly, the van hit a bump that jerked Jen's hand upward, causing her to scream at the overweight driver sitting beside her. "God damn it, Tony! Where the hell did you learn to drive?"

Tony lowered his head while still trying to keep his eyes on the road. "This is New York, Ms. Thompson. The roads here suck."

"Says the man who can eat a whole ice cream behind the wheel without spilling it," said Jen before turning her focus back to applying her makeup. "Now our van is going to be first on the scene so act fast. We're getting a real eyewitness story. Don't screw it up."

Tony nodded with his head still slumped over. "Yes, Ms. Thompson."

She then shut the compact and placed it inside a makeup kit between the seats. "Remember, the building is just as important as me. So try to get some shots of it, too. But not too many that people forget I'm there. Got it?"

Tony didn't respond as he pulled up to a small group of

people crowding the road. The curious onlookers were all standing in front of a federal police barricade of cop cars, blocking off an area directly in front of a derelict building with half the top floor missing.

Jen and Tony both exited the van and opened up the back doors. Jennifer grabbed her microphone and immediately spotted a federal police officer she recognized attempting to calm the crowd. "Tony, follow me."

Tony picked up his camera and threw it over his shoulder, struggling to keep up with Jen as she pushed her way through the crowd. "Hey, Jim! Jim! Over here."

Annoyed to see her, the police officer lifted his hand and turned to walk away from the eager reporter. "Not now, Jennifer. You're the last person I want to see."

"Oh, come on," she nagged, as she reached the front of the crowd. "Don't tell me you're still mad?"

Unable to resist arguing, the cop stomped back over to her, shaking his head. "You used me, Jen. I called you like five times since that night."

"You're a married man," said Jennifer, her voice overly soft and understanding. "I didn't want to get you caught."

He stared her down with two fierce eyes. "You're right. I'm a married man. So leave me alone."

Still standing in front of her, Jim began focusing his attention to the rest of the crowd as Jen continued to plead with him. "Just tell me something. Anything. Like is this connected to that gas station explosion from earlier?"

"No comment," he said, refusing to look at her.

"Fine." Jen stood tall and brought her hands to her hips, shifting her demeanor from sweet to threatening. "Then I'll just have a little chat with your wife tonight."

She turned to walk away when Jim nervously called out to her. "You wouldn't..."

He was too frightened to say the words out loud, and the cutthroat reporter, looking back over her shoulder, sensed an opportunity looming. "All I want is a little taste. That's all."

"Fine," said the irritated officer. "But you're not going to believe me."

She approached him again with a smile on her face. "Let me worry about that."

With the crowd focused on the abandoned building behind him, the cop cautiously looked around before leaning closer to Jen and whispering. "Witnesses called in saying the top floor of the building just blew up out of nowhere. Then a patrol car showed up and saw a man flying around the building."

Skeptical, Jennifer looked at him sideways. "Jimmy, you told me you were going to stop smoking that crap."

"I'm serious."

"You're an asshole, you know that?" She turned and began walking away. "Expect a call from your wife."

"No!" shouted Jim, weakly reaching out to her. "Please, Jennifer. I—"

His sentence was cut off by a loud crash from inside the building. Distracted, they both looked up to see a man propel himself out of the roof like a rocket and into the blue sky. The people in the crowd pointed and watched in awe as the man flew higher and higher until disappearing completely in the clouds.

The vindicated officer turned back to Jennifer, who was already halfway through the crowd. "See! I told you."

Ecstatic, she ran up to him but kept her eyes locked on the building ahead. "Oh, my God, Jimmy! I love you!"

He warily took a step back with his hands out, eager to distance himself from the woman. "Okay. Just don't let my wife find out."

Jennifer turned to the edge of the crowd, where Tony patiently waited with the camera on his shoulder. "Tony, get ready."

Surprised, he scrambled to put on the headset that had been draped around his neck. "We're going live now?"

"Yes," said Jennifer, lifting up the microphone while stretching out her shoulders.

With one hand clinging to the camera on his shoulder, Tony used the other to press the headset against his ear. "But the studio isn't—"

Jen lowered the microphone to burst out in a fit of anger. "Just tell them we're ready!"

Shaking his head with a sigh, Tony readied his stance and focused the camera on the reporter with the building in the background. "Ok. We're good to go. Live in five…four…three…"

Jennifer quickly fluffed the edges of her hair before forcing out a fake smile "Good afternoon. This is Jennifer Thompson reporting live from Harlem where federal officers have just reported to investigate an explosion that partially destroyed the building behind me. No word yet on whether its related to the gas station explosion from earlier today. But when the police arrived on scene they discovered a man flying around the building without ropes, wires, or supports of any kind. Honestly, I didn't believe them when they told me. Until I saw it for myself just a moment ago. A man shot through the building's roof and flew up into the sky. Yes, folks, he was flying."

She continued to talk as Tony moved the camera to focus on the building. "We don't know if this is terrorism, but whoever is responsible for—"

Jennifer was interrupted by another explosion that erupted out the side of the building. From within the blast, a man shot out through the green flames and Tony followed him with the camera as the man slammed into the street, creating a small crater in the pavement.

As a large cloud of dust cleared away from the area, Tony zoomed in on the hole while Jennifer resumed her report. "I… uh…oh, jeez. Another explosion just blew a man into the street and left a giant hole in the ground. I don't see a body, but there's no way anybody could've survived—Wait! Someone's coming out of the building."

Tony shifted the camera back to the building and focused in on the three commandos walking out the front door. "It appears to be three heavily armed individuals wearing what looks like some kind of body armor. A woman is leading two men towards the hole and…"

As soon as she reached the edge, Wolf aimed her M4 into the crater only to have an energy blast knock it from her hands. Adam dove up from from inside the crater, his clothes shredded to tatters, and knocked the stunned girl straight back. Stopping himself in mid-air after the collision with Wolf, Adam then spun around, simultaneously kicking the grenade launcher and rifle out of Colt and Raptor's hands.

Adam landed gracefully on his feet after the gravity-defying move and turned to the two unarmed soldiers. Raptor immediately took a fighting stance, but Colt breathed deep, slowly raising his fists while staring Adam down. "I never did like you."

The super soldier stood tall and unafraid with his arms at his sides. "I never asked you to."

Raptor and Colt attacked in perfect synchronization, alternating kicks and punches for a relentless assault, but even flawless precision was no match for the super soldier. Adam slowly backed up in the middle of the street, easily maneuvering with lightning speed around every strike thrown at him. He was toying with them, practically dancing through their attacks as Colt grew frustrated at the amazing speed of his former commander.

In a desperate plea to land a blow, Raptor charged ahead to tackle his opponent, but Adam casually moved to the side, allowing Raptor's momentum to send him flying past. The super soldier then released a blast of energy into Raptor's back, lighting his attacker up in flames. Flailing his arms around in panic, Raptor dropped to the ground screaming, but the momentary distraction allowed Colt the chance to grab Adam from behind and hold a shiny green knife to his throat. "This is for Fox."

Adam was caught off guard from the pain as the blade dug into his skin. It felt strange, almost comforting, to have the warm trickle of blood drip down his neck, but Adam fought back and prevented the knife from going any further. In one swift motion, Adam elbowed Colt in the stomach, grabbed him by the throat, and lifted him straight off the ground. "His name was Travis."

With a quick flick of the wrist, Colt's neck snapped like a twig and Adam dropped the limp corpse to the pavement. He then turned around to find the barrel of an MK 23 pistol staring back at him. Behind the gun, Wolf's panicked finger nervously pressed against the trigger but stopped short of squeezing it. Casually taking a deep breath, Adam looked around at the barricade of cop cars on both sides of him. Hiding behind the cars was a small army of policemen, all nervously aiming their weapons at him yet too hesitant to fire. Further behind them were huge crowds of civilians and news crews, eagerly watching and waiting to see how the scene would unfold.

After taking it all in, Adam turned back to Wolf. "What are you doing, Sarah?"

Holding it with one hand, she clenched onto the gun's handle, but still, her finger anxiously shook on the trigger. "I thought I told you not to call me that."

"Look around you," said Adam, spreading his arms out wide to the audience surrounding them. "Are you really going to kill me in front of all these people on global television? You're not a murderer, Sarah. This is not who you are."

She brought her other hand up to hold the weapon's grip even tighter. "I don't care."

Staring into her eyes, Adam slowly shook his head. "I know you don't want to kill me, Sarah…"

"Stop saying my name!"

"…otherwise you would've already pulled the trigger."

"Just shut up!" she screamed, clenching her face as her eyes started to swell.

Adam stood still, never blinking or looking away. "No."

"Shut your mouth!" Wolf's entire arms shook as the building tears seeped out from within her eyes. "Don't you say another goddamn word."

"I know you're scared, Sarah. Me too." Raising his arm up slowly, Adam placed a hand on top of the gun and began lowering it back down. "It's okay to be scared."

The emotional wall Wolf had been holding back collapsed as she fell forward, crying into Adam's arms. "You left me, Adam. I was alone."

He held her tight and spoke softly into her ear. "I know."

"I loved you and you just left me." She buried her head into his chest, unable to stop her hysterical sobs. "I was by myself. I had no one."

Adam shook his head, fighting to keep the guilt at bay. "Please...please don't cry."

"I already have. All those nights without you. I missed you so much. Why did you leave me?"

He opened his mouth but found his throat too dry to speak, so he forced the words to come out, cracked and hoarse. "I had to. I'm sorry. But I promise...you will never be alone again. Not anymore."

Wolf looked up from within Adam's arms and he stared down into her eyes, red and swollen from the tears pouring down her cheeks. "This was my fault. I know that. But eyes so beautiful shouldn't be filled with such sadness. I can make it right. I can take it all away. All you have to do is let me."

In the three years since he left The Armory, Adam had often wondered about this moment. He contemplated what he would do to the only woman in the world his heart ever yearned for and found deciding the fate of humanity was a lot easier when love wasn't standing in his way. Ultimately, Adam left the decision to her, so he looked down and waited for a response. She didn't say a word, though. Wolf simply closed her eyes and laid her head back down onto his chest.

That was all the answer he needed.

Smiling, Adam held her tight as a wave of fire slowly emanated from his body. "Goodbye, my love."

He continued to bask in her embrace while the flaming surge grew and grew until they were completely engulfed and Wolf burned away to ash.

# 44

Tony's hands shook as he struggled to keep the camera steady. He zoomed in on the two individuals in the flames and watched horrified while the young woman's body crumbled to dust and blew away in the wind.

Standing beside him, Jennifer continued to report what she was seeing, her voice trembling and afraid. "Oh, my God. I don't...I can't possibly believe what's happening. This man...I don't know if he's even a man, but whatever he is...has just completely burned a woman away to nothing. I don't know what to say. I...I'm nearly speechless. And I believe he's coming this way."

As the flames dwindled around his body, the naked man approached the barricade of cop cars as one of the frightened officers jerked his gun forward. "F...f—freeze right there! Don't come any closer or I'll...I mean we...we will shoot!"

The man stopped ten paces from the cars. Tony, as well as the other cameramen scattered throughout the crowd, focused in on him while the bystanders, whispering amongst themselves, stared on in amazement.

The man then held out his arms and the commotion ceased as he began to speak. "Ladies and gentlemen of the world, don't be afraid. I'm not here for your fear. Only your salvation. As a child, I felt nothing for the pain of humanity because I didn't think it mattered, but today I know differently. I'm not a god as many of you are assuming, but I'm more human now than I've been my whole life. Like all of you, I'm a slave to emotion. Chained by pride, love, anger, even hate. But as I journeyed the earth there was only one thing constant in my soul: pity. I pitied myself as well as every other human brought into this world, ripped from the womb of enlightenment and thrown into a planet of suffering and destruction. Well that changes now. No longer shall the suffering cry themselves to sleep at dusk hoping they didn't wake come dawn. No longer shall the corrupt and arrogant prey on the weak and painful. No longer shall this failed experiment called sentience be a plague upon the planet. I'm not here to end life. I'm here to set it free. So let this moment be the end to the age of Man and the beginning to the era of a new species free from an existence of paradox. Free from the mind, free from the heart, and free from the gods of Man."

With his arms still spread out wide, the man looked up to the sky and closed his eyes as sparks of electricity flared around his body and two flames formed in his open palms. The crowd then gasped in unison as two lines of fire shot from the man's hands and slammed into the buildings around them, sending debris and rubble flying to the streets below.

Erupting in panic, the crowd turned to a frantic stampede as it started to run in the opposite direction. Waves of fire continued to blast through the buildings, and the cops turned to join the mob fleeing for their lives. From behind them, two consecutive explosions from underneath the cop cars launched the vehicles flying overhead before splattering the crowd below.

Tony lowered his camera but held onto it while huffing and puffing out of breath to keep up with the people pushing him forward.

Jennifer was several steps in front of him and tried to keep the microphone to her face while talking in between breaths. "I'm still here. Running now as this...thing is attacking us. I'm going to try and talk for as long as possible. There's explosions and debris falling all around me. Everyone is panicking. Move, people! Just go!"

As the horde desperately pushed ahead, Tony was shoved from behind and fell face first into the street. His camera flew from his hand and landed amidst the crowd, shattering against the pavement. The crashing noise drew Jen's attention and she looked back just in time to watch her cameraman stomped to death under an army of marching boots. "Tony!"

Tossing aside the microphone, Jen forced her way back through the frenzied mob and dropped to her knees, futilely trying to push the herd of fleeing people away from Tony's crumpled body. "Get away! Move it! Can't you see he's hurt!?"

Distraught, Jen lifted up his head, crushed and mangled beyond recognition, as a flood of tears ran down her face. An ooze of blood seeped out onto her hands and she reflexively dropped the cameraman's head in horror. A woman then screamed beside her and Jennifer looked up to find a giant chunk of concrete falling straight towards them.

# 45

From his back, Tyran looked around at the lab assistants, all nearly half his age, strapping him down to the cold, metal operating table with thick, iron restraints. He was in a basement, dark, damp and lit by a single bulb flickering at the end of its life. The concrete walls and ceiling stained with black mold were a stark contrast from the million dollar lab equipment surrounding him, none of which he could identify.

All Tyran knew was that his patience was wearing thin. "What's the hold up? Let's get this show on the road."

Barely older than his assistants, the head scientist with slicked black hair walked over to him holding a rather large syringe filled with golden fluid. "Are you sure about this? Once I inject you with phase one of the procedure there's no turning back."

"Just do it," said Tyran without hesitation.

The man reluctantly nodded his head. "Ok. But it's your funeral."

The assistants stepped back to the outskirts of the room as the scientist carefully plunged the needle into Tyran's arm. He then removed it and stood back, waiting for several silent seconds before Tyran began awkwardly squirming in his restraints. "It...burns. Like nothing I've ever felt before."

He gradually grinded his teeth harder and harder, grunting to resist the pain growing more intense by the second. His body tensed up, bulging thick veins from his arms and neck while thin streams of blood flowed into his eyes.

Sensing something was wrong, the scientist turned and pointed to an assistant. "Get the beta blockers! Quick! Before his heart gives out."

Tyran abruptly ripped his arm free from the iron restraint and grabbed ahold of the scientist's lab coat. "No! Keep going!"

Dropping the syringe to the floor, the scientist went limp in Tyran's grasp. "You're about to go into cardiac arrest. We need to stop."

"Finish it!" screamed Tyran, practically spitting in the man's face. "Give me it all!"

He released his hold on the frazzled scientist, who then lowered his head and walked over to a junction box on the wall. He put his hand on a large switch connected to the box and looked back at Tyran one last time before pulling it down.

Several machines positioned around the room sent surges of electricity into thick cables sprawled across the floor and into the operating table. The currents ran up and down the metal, shocking Tyran's flesh, which then absorbed every jolt. His body began to convulse, blood seeping out from his eyes, ears, and nose. The scientist's jaw dropped in horror and he watched on while muttering in Russian under his breath.

Tyran howled a blood curdling scream and everyone in the room cringed to cover their ears. One of machines overloaded, exploding into a thousand pieces while the others sent sparks flying around the room. The single dim light swaying above the table shattered, covering the room in darkness except for the intermittent flashes of electricity dancing across Tyran's body.

Having had enough, the frightened scientist scurried back to the junction box next to him. "It's too much too fast. I'm shutting it down."

"No!" screamed Tyran, ripping his other arm free from its restraint. "I need more."

He reached out and fired an energy blast at the scientist, striking him in the back and sending his body soaring to the other side of the room.

Tyran then let loose a devious laugh as more electricity rushed into him. The terrified assistants scurried towards the basement's only door, fleeing for their lives. Before they could escape though, a large burst of flames erupted from Tyran's body, engulfing the room and collapsing the entire concrete ceiling down on top of them.

# 46

After watching the footage of New York City's utter and complete destruction, there wasn't much in terms of rational thought racing through Hopkins's mind. Survival instinct took over his body as he retreated to his bedroom and immediately began packing a bag.

Despite his lavish office, Hopkins's dormitory was no different than anyone else's in The Armory. The room was stark and completely lacking in character. Although bland, the simple design made organization a cinch, allowing Hopkins to pack his things as quickly as possible.

Hurriedly focused on the task, Hopkins paid no attention to Jason and Christine as they quietly entered the room. Christine carefully shut the door behind them and Jason walked over to stare down at the bag nearly half filled with clothes on the bed. "Where are you headed?"

Hopkins answered while continuing to pack. "Far away from here. I suggest you do the same."

Jason shook his head. "We aren't going anywhere and neither are you."

Hopkins stopped and finally turned to face them. "He's coming here and, personally, I don't want to be around when he arrives."

"It won't matter," said Christine, stepping up to stand by Jason's side. "He'll find you."

Ignoring her prediction, Hopkins resumed packing the bag, eager to place blame for their situation. "I told you to find him and stop him. This is as much my fault as it is yours."

"You're incapable of taking responsibility for your actions, aren't you?" Jason moved over, blocking Hopkins's path. "You gave him the power to do this. You made him what he is. Adam is your creation, and now you're just going to pack your bags and run?"

Annoyed, Hopkins pushed him aside to approach the bed. "A crazed super soldier is flying around the world killing everything he sees and the last place I want to be is the house he grew up in. I'm leaving."

He zipped the bag closed, picked it up, and started towards the door when this time it was Christine who stepped in his way. "We can't leave."

He angrily stared her down. "Move out of my way, Christine."

"No," she replied to the demand, stern and unwavering.

Hopkins went to move around her, but again, Christine stepped in front of him. He then let out a hard, aggravated sigh. "This is childish. Get out of my way."

Jason walked up beside him. "It's over, Hopkins. All of us failed Adam and now it's time to face what we've done."

Furious, Hopkins threw the bag on the floor. "I'm not letting some psychopath kill me just because he's filled with deluded righteousness. I'm going to live through this and—"

A loud boom jolted the entire room, which then shook and rumbled continuously. Jason and Hopkins fell to the floor while Christine stayed on her feet, stumbling over to hold onto a wall. "What...what's going on?"

Scared and anxious, Hopkins carefully balanced himself to get to his feet in the trembling room. "What do you think? He's here. Now it's definitely time to go."

Without waiting for the analysts to catch up, Hopkins bolted for the door and left the room, where a panicked crowd ran back and forth through the vibrating hallway. He pushed his way through the mob, fighting to stay upright on the quaking floor.

Turning a corner, the tremors suddenly stopped and Hopkins was met with an explosion that blew a hole right through the wall beside him. He was knocked to the floor, covered in a pile of rubble and debris. A cloud of thick dust entered his lungs, causing Hopkins to cough as he tried to sit up. His attention, frightened yet focused, was then drawn upwards as a dark figure stepped through the hole in the wall. "We both know what you came to do. Just kill me and get it over with."

The figure approached and Hopkins's eyes grew wide in shock. The light had revealed Tyran's scarred face staring down at him. "I'm not going kill you, Jack. I'll save that pleasure for someone else."

# 47

Once New York was destroyed, Adam swept down the east coast razing the ground in his path. He was met with some resistance along the way. Brave private citizens who took up arms as well as a rapidly mobilized army daring to put up a fight. They fought valiantly. They died even more so.

From there he moved west and was surprised to have encountered some of the rumored projects under Hopkins's supervision. Although they had yet to be deployed in actual combat, there was gossip that the nano-tech swarm and bi-pedal battle tank were functionally operational. During his campaign, the weapons ambushed Adam in Kansas and Colorado, respectively. The nano-swarm was unlike anything he had faced before, tiny flying robots that smothered every inch of his body, but they burned up like flies after a single blast of energy. Likewise, the battle tank's hide was resilient, able to withstand even the strongest of Adam's attacks. It was slow, however, and the super soldier simply flew around the machine in circles until finding a weak spot for him to exploit.

Continuing his crusade, Adam soared over the empty Nevadan desert when a trail of rising smoke in the distance caught his attention. He sped up to the source and quickly realized the scenery seemed vaguely familiar. That's when he looked down and saw a giant hole in the desert floor leading directly into The Armory.

Adam flew down into the smoked filled pit and entered the hallways, which had become a cavernous system of cramped tunnels. Rubble and debris covered every inch of floor with flames sporadically raging throughout the underground facility he once called home. Adam floated off the ground as he continued to head deeper, passing by a never-ending parade of bodies everywhere he went.

Eventually, the super soldier recognized a face among the corpses and he dropped to a knee beside it, carefully caressing the side of her lifeless face. "Christine…"

He closed his eyes and took a deep, mournful breath while holding her head close to his chest.

"I never thought seeing a dead body could have that effect on you," said a familiar voice calling to him from inside a room.

His concentration broken, Adam followed the man's words into the room where he discovered Jason pinned to the back wall by a metal rod impaled through his abdomen.

"Jason, who did this?" asked Adam, approaching the doomed man slowly.

Jason hacked out a dry, wheezy cough and his battered, bloody face twisted as he struggled to speak. "It was Tyran."

Adam's stern expression widened into a look of surprise. "How?"

"He had your powers." Jason painfully swallowed before continuing on. "Molotok must have finally made their super solider. Ironic it had to be him."

Adam could feel his hand clenching into a fist on its own. "Where did he go?"

"I…I don't know."

Adam reached forward and gently wiped the blood from Jason's brow. "It wasn't supposed to be like this. I was supposed to be the only one."

Jason's tired and weak face faintly smiled. "And what makes you so different from him?"

"Whether you understand it or not," said Adam, still cleaning the blood from Jason's forehead, "I am saving humanity. All Tyran wants is war and conflict, but I will not let him turn this world into an eternal battlefield."

"No, Adam. You just want to make it into a graveyard."

With Jason's face as clean as it could get, Adam stopped wiping and smirked. "There's a difference."

"But is one better than the other?" asked Jason.

"Yes," answered Adam as he grabbed the metal bar protruding from Jason's body and jammed it deeper into his abdomen. "Because only one can know peace."

Spitting out blood, Jason let out a final gasp of life before going limp and falling forward against the rod still impaling him to the wall.

# 48

Upon leaving The Armory, Adam followed a trail west of smoke and devastation. He passed mostly small towns with pockets of dense civilization. The scenes weren't all that dissimilar from the ones he left in his own sweeping destruction of the country, but with one distinct difference. He could hear the cries of survivors weeping from underneath the rubble. Tyran didn't want to end people's suffering. He was only interested in pain, forcing Adam to finish the job as he continued across the land.

As the sun fell beneath the skyline, the desolation eventually led Adam back to Los Angeles, a familiar city with painful memories. Large clouds of dust floated overtop the barren, dimly lit streets, unable to mask the stench of death from wafting through the air. Bodies and debris were strewn across every downtown intersection, where Adam found Tyran standing on a rooftop and firing random blasts of energy at the buildings surrounding him.

Flying towards him at full speed, Adam came to a sudden stop before landing on an adjacent roof. Tyran then smiled and yelled out to his fellow super soldier from across the way. "You finally found me."

"Your stench is hard to miss," Adam taunted back.

Amused by the comment, Tyran simply shrugged his shoulders. "Well, I did just spend the last three years in a Russian jungle."

Adam casually floated up and across the street to join Tyran on his rooftop. "So what? You're Molotok's super soldier now?"

Tyran's head rocked backwards, laughing hysterically. "I'm

not any kind of soldier. Their job is to take orders, and I think people like us are above that now."

Adam stared Tyran down, perturbed by his cackling. "I'm nothing like you."

"On the contrary," Tyran replied while approaching the young super soldier. "I saw what you did in New York. Impressive stuff."

Adam debated for a moment whether the comment was even worthy of a response. He could've spent all night up on this rooftop, exchanging words back and forth with a power driven sociopath, but that would've been pointless. Any discussion would've only led them to one conclusion, so Adam spread his legs into a fighting stance and raised his fists ready for battle.

Tyran didn't feel the same way, though. He snorted while waving off Adam's seriousness. "Put your hands down, son. There's no need for us to fight."

"I've been training with these powers a lot longer than you have," said Adam, holding strong and firm in the same position. "Trust me. It wouldn't be a fight."

Tyran smirked and held the expression for several seconds before quickly jabbing Adam straight in the jaw. The sucker punch sent Adam soaring backwards off the roof and slamming into an office building several blocks over. The entire structure collapsed in on itself, erupting a giant plume of dust from the ruins.

Tyran then casually floated over and landed on a roof across the street. "Oh, come on," he shouted. "Get up. I know you can take more than that."

The rubble slowly moved as Adam emerged out from under it, his fists clenched and bearing his teeth. He swiftly lifted his hands, unleashing a large blast of energy up towards the rooftop. Tyran barely managed to jump out of the way as the strong wave shot through the top half of the building, instantly vaporizing it into dust.

Adam then propelled himself from the wreckage, soaring towards Tyran and tackling him at full speed. Locked into one another, the two super soldiers spiraled through the air as Adam speared his opponent straight into a towering skyscraper. Half the building broke away, plummeting to the ground below, but only Adam emerged out the other side.

Floating high in the air, Adam stopped and turned back to the partially destroyed skyscraper, waiting for Tyran to reveal himself. After a few seconds, Adam's attention was drawn upwards, and he looked to find Tyran coming down at him feet first. Adam barely dodged the attack and retaliated with a punch, but Tyran blocked that as well, countering with another attack of his own.

With lightning fast reflexes, the two super soldiers relentlessly went after one another. Floating around in circles, they exchanged kicks and punches high above the city streets, endlessly engaged in brutal combat.

Breaking away slightly for an opening, Adam came back with a quick jab, but Tyran grabbed his fist, catching the attack before it had a chance to land. He then flashed Adam a cocky wink with his scarred eye before spinning around and throwing him over his shoulder, down towards the ground below.

As Adam hopelessly plunged towards the street, he looked back to regain his balance only to find a huge energy wave gaining on him. He tried to stop but it was too late. The blast overtook him, engulfing his body and slamming him into an elevated freeway lined with abandoned vehicles.

The entire road collapsed into a jumbled mess of twisted metal and concrete. Bloody and bruised, Adam slowly rose to his feet amidst the debris and shook the ringing from his head.

Tyran then landed atop the mountain of rubble and looked down at his foe with an obnoxious grin. "Wow. You look terrible. That must've hurt."

Adam struggled to his feet as Tyran walked down the mound to approach him. He then threw a weak series of punches that Tyran easily blocked and followed up with an assault of his own. Tired and worn, Adam futilely tried to evade the attack but it was useless. Tyran eventually overtook Adam's feeble defense and knocked him down to his hands and knees.

He then lightly kicked Adam over onto his back and placed a firm foot on top of his chest. "How does the world look from down there, my boy?"

Adam fought against Tyran's leg pinning him to the ground but was unable to move it. "How did you...get so...strong?"

Tyran towered over Adam, smiling down at him. "You're rusty. That's all. It's been a while since you had a real challenge."

"But I...I..."

"Oh, stop it," Tyran casually joked, lifting his foot from Adam's chest. "Everyone could use a good beating once in a while."

Now free, Adam rolled over onto his side, coughing up blood as he tried to speak. "What do you want?"

Tyran crouched down to Adam's eye level. "I want what you want: to save humanity. With our powers we can rebuild the world as it was meant to be. We can mold it the way we want. Together, we can create any future we desire. All you have to do is join me."

Adam looked up to sneer at him, his lips covered in blood. "Go to hell."

"I did," Tyran said with a smile. "Who do you think made me this way?"

Tyran then stood back up and loomed over his fallen opponent. "I'll give you one day to think about it. That should be plenty of time to realize this crusade of genocide you're on is pointless. Once you've come to a decision meet me at Yoyogi Park in Tokyo. I'll be waiting."

Tyran turned to walk away, only managing to get a few steps before Adam called to him. "Why Japan?"

He stopped and barely looked over his shoulder to answer. "Because I have an old friend there just dying to see you."

Adam then watched as Tyran launched himself off the rubble, flying off into the night's sky before disappearing in the darkness.

# 49

The sun had risen on the ruined city by the time Adam regained enough strength to stand. He felt weak and sore but not nearly as hurt as he should've been thanks to his powers.

Finally rising to his feet, the morning light allowed Adam to properly survey Los Angeles's devastation. Only half of the city's skyline remained. The other half was either ravaged beyond repair or engulfed in flames. Blood stained rubble and debris covered the ground, mixed with bodies torn to shreds. Lots and lots of bodies. None of them moving.

In a moment, the Apocalyptic sight was completely gone from Adam's mind and he took off flying into the distance.

Adam didn't know exactly where he was headed. He just found water and kept on blindly soaring through the air, weaving in and out of the clouds for what seemed like hundreds of miles with nothing but the empty seas beneath him. The first time he left Los Angeles, all those years ago, Adam spent days wandering the sky without ever touching the ground. He felt free back then, lost in the thin atmosphere and rays of pure, unfiltered sunshine.

Now he had a purpose and that time of wanton apathy was behind him. Yet still, a small part of Adam wished he could shed his powers and the responsibility that came with them. He asked himself why he couldn't have just been a normal kid with a normal father and a normal life.

It was only a brief moment of doubt, though, for another trail of billowing smoke snapped him back to reality.

Quickly veering left, Adam continued on over the ocean, descending as fast as he could go. At first he thought it might've been a large ship, possibly a freighter, on fire way off in the distance, but land started quickly coming into view along the horizon.

It was an island, mostly barren by the looks of it, and the smoke was rising into the sky from a mountaintop. Adam didn't understand why Tyran would stop here of all places, but when he dropped down to glide above the mountain's craggy surface, Adam realized where the smoke was coming from.

As he reached the peak, Adam floated over a cliff edge and looked down into a deep crater filled with bubbling lava, alive and churning. The volcano was mesmerizing, and, similar to when he was in the clouds, Adam lost himself while staring into the molten rock, as if his very soul was on fire.

He eventually regained enough of his senses to realize that he'd just been floating there, alone and hypnotized by frothy magma, but instead of flying away, Adam floated down and sat atop a small plateau overlooking the lava pit below.

Not for the first time, the super soldier contemplated never moving again, simply staying in that spot forever until the world did with him what it wished. He took a deep breath, hoping that decision would be made for him, but a familiar voice from behind stole away his self-pity. "Halemaumau crater."

Adam glanced over his shoulder and was not surprised to find Travis standing behind him. Rather than say hello to his dead friend though, Adam just turned back around to stare into the volcano.

Undeterred by the snub, Travis walked up to stand alongside him. "That's what it's called."

"I didn't ask," said Adam, still refusing to look up at his visitor.

Travis bent down to pick a handful of dark crystals off the ground and dropped them over the edge into the lava below. "In Hawaiin mythology, it's said to be the home of Madame Pele, a Fire Godess also known as the earth-eating woman."

"You have a point?" asked Adam, slightly annoyed.

Sitting down next him, Travis casually shook his head. "No. Not really."

Adam let out a sigh as he lowered his head in frustration.

"You told me I was chosen, Travis. That I was given this power for a reason. How did you know? Who told you?"

Comfortable with his feet dangling over the cliff, Travis leaned back onto his hands to relax. "Someone's been watching you and guiding you the way she wants. But you've strayed from the path she intended."

Curious, Adam finally turned to look at his deceased friend. "Are you talking about that old woman? She's using me?"

Travis answered silently by slowly nodding his head. Adam then turned to look back out over the creater. "And what about Tyran? Was he chosen too?"

Travis nonchalantly shrugged his shoulders. "Perhaps."

"Perhaps?" repeated Adam, almost insulted by the vague response. "That's all you've got for me?"

Travis shook his head with a grimace. "I don't have all the answers, Adam."

Dejected, Adam leaned forward, slumping his shoulders. "So what do I do then?"

Travis leaned forward, as well, and placed a hand on Adam's shoulder. "It's your power. You choose what to do with it."

Adam rolled his eyes at the cryptic response as Travis began to stand. "Gee. Thanks for the advice."

"She chose you, Adam. Why and what she's planning I have no idea. But what I do know is that you need to stop asking why. Just accept the facts and do what you believe is right."

Adam looked up as Travis offered his final, parting words while slowly backing away. "Life isn't about finding a purpose, Adam. It's about following your heart. Make the decision, take a step forward, and never look back."

A slight wind blew across the mountiantop and Travis's figure slowly faded with the breeze. Once his friend had vanished into the air, Adam stood with his feet teetering over the edge of the cliff. He then took a deep breath, fell forward, and plummetted straight down through the volcano, plunging head first into the smoldering lava on the crater floor.

# 50

Every nation around the globe responded differently to Adam's attack on America. Although the crazed super soldier had yet to strike any other country, the world's governments weren't taking any chances. Adam spoke of humanity as a whole, not individual peoples. The leaders all assumed it would only be a matter of time before they were next on the maniac's hit list. The one thing they weren't doing, though, was working together.

A traditionally isolated nation, Japan managed to largely avoid the global economic collapse by turning inward. That same strategy, however, would prove futile when dealing with a crazed super soldier. Their whole country was a series of islands, after all. They didn't have many places to hide.

Studying Adam's systematic destruction of the American coastline, Japanese leaders noticed that the super soldier was focusing on large cities, targeting dense populations in order to reach the most amount of people in the shortest amount of time. That thought in mind, Japan had begun evacuating the country's urban centers, dispersing its people to spread out across the countryside, and with a population of over fourteen million, Tokyo's large scale evacuation was unprecedented.

On the outskirts of the sprawling Asian metropolis, armed members of Japan's Self-Defense Force carefully yet quickly directed the last of the evacuating civilians away from the city. Tanks, trucks, and armored ground troops lined the suburban streets as millions of ordinary citizens turned refugees jammed together like a herd of sheep mindlessly pushing their way forward.

Suddenly, a gust of wind rushed through the caravan, interrupting the calmness of the crisp blue day. The breeze picked up all around the anxious crowd and the evacuees, every one of which was already on edge, paused to look around confused. An eerie hush settled over the Tokyo air usually vibrant and filled with life.

The tense moment of silence lasted several seconds until a soldier spotted a small yet unnatural speck in the distant sky. He pointed up and yelled out, nervously directing everyone's attention to the rapidly approaching dot. Even before the object came into view, the soldiers surrounding the large mass of people in the street all raised their weapons to aim at it. But by the time the figure took the shape of a man, it was already too late.

The super soldier fearlessly flew at full speed head first into the armored tank leading the convoy. The collision sent out a booming shockwave in every direction that knocked the crowd to the ground as the massive tank crumpled in on itself like a feeble tin can. It took a moment for both the evacuees and soldiers to recover back to their feet. When they looked up, they saw Adam for the first time standing tall and glorious atop a contorted pile of metal.

He was different than how he appeared on the television, though. In New York City, he gave his speech as a naked individual. Now every inch of his body was coated in a thin layer of dark, jagged rock that hugged his frame tightly like an extra layer of skin. The only sign of the flesh underneath were breaks by his eyes and mouth where the stone wrapped around his face like a mask.

Adam was undoubtedly a scary, intimidating sight, but the soldiers' commander refused to cower in fear. He yelled out an order and his scattered troops instantly opened fire at the menacing super soldier. The loud pop of gunfire ignited a spark within the horde of civilians, causing the crowd to push and shove in all directions.

Leaving his elevated position, Adam swiftly floated away only to turn around and fly back the way he came. The scared citizens dispersed from the convoy, fleeing for their lives as the soldiers continued to fire their weapons. Rolling side to side mid-flight, Adam easily dodged the onslaught of bullets while approaching them. He then passed overhead and fired two quick blasts into the crowd before continuing on his way.

The already frantic evacuees pushed harder and faster to put distance between themselves and the firing troops. As the soldiers ran out of ammo, they all began to reload together but not fast enough. Adam had turned around and was already on top of them for another pass, firing two more shots that sent bodies and debris flying through the air.

A wave of dust rushed out in all directions, consuming the scared citizens and whatever squadron of troops were left. Adam didn't stop, though. He remained hovering above the street, firing blast after blast at whatever few stragglers remained until the neighborhood had become nothing short of a wasteland. Once he was satisfied by the lack of movement below, Adam floated away from the wreckage and slowly drifted to a park on the far side of the city.

He landed on a street corner just outside the park's entrance and surveyed the abandoned meadow before him. Strong, radiant sunlight beamed down through the cloudless sky, lighting up the park's lush green trees and serene pond. Satisfied by the emptiness, Adam walked through the entrance arch and across a field of grass towards the center of the park. There he found Hopkins seated slumped over on a bench, battered and bleeding with his suit in tatters.

The man stared blankly ahead and didn't even bother moving his eyes to look as Adam casually sat down next to him. "Hello, Hopkins."

Hopkins's exhausted head bobbed as if it were a struggle just to hold it up. "Go screw yourself."

Adam smirked while staring out at the beautifully tranquil park. "I see Tyran had some fun with you."

"But didn't kill me." Hopkins managed to tilt his head ever so slightly in Adam's direction, the most he could do to look at him. "He was saving that job for someone he thought was more deserving."

Adam nodded. "I can see that."

"It doesn't matter anyway," Hopkins muttered barely louder than a whisper. "You can't survive the Fifth Horseman. I built it specifically for you, so just kill me and get it over with."

Although the first part of his comment intrigued him, Adam focused more on mocking him with the second. "I haven't seen you in three years and that's all you can say? 'Kill me and get it over with?' I would never. Then I'd miss this wonderful opportunity to reminisce about old times."

Hopkins took a deep, pained breath, sulking even further into the bench. "When I first saw you I never pictured it coming to this. I thought you were just some unlucky, punk kid caught up in our world. But you weren't. You were actually born for it and amazed me every step of the way. Which was probably why I never liked you."

"Touching," said Adam, rolling his eyes.

Ignoring the sarcastic comment, Hopkins continued to ruminate. "But Martinez was never amazed. From the moment he saw you, he knew you were something special. He knew that you had greatness within you. It's too bad you used it for such horrible things."

Adam smiled, chuckling to himself. "You want to talk about horrible things? That's a laugh. The only person you ever cared about was yourself."

"Myself?" asked Hopkins, managing to express offense despite his poor condition. "I did what I did for the sake of my country. I was going to give America the tools we needed to survive the war."

Adam stood from the bench and turned to face his former boss. "You created the war instead."

Hopkins then summoned whatever energy he had left to lift his face, covered in bruises, and stare Adam in his eyes. "No. I didn't start this fight. I just created the monster who did."

"I'm not a monster..." Adam raised his hand and fired a single blast that completely consumed the frail man sitting before him. "...I'm human."

When the blast faded, Hopkins and the bench were engulfed in flames, and Adam watched as the heat melted away the corpse's flesh and burned its bones to dust.

He could sense Tyran approaching him from behind but didn't bother turning around. The sight before him was too entertaining to look away.

Instead, Adam remained still as Tyran reached out with a fist and gave two succinct knocks to the rocky plate coating Adam's back. "This is a good look for you. Where'd you get it?"

"I took your advice and went to hell," said Adam, finally turning around to look his rival in the eye.

Tyran smiled, pleasantly surprised by the boy's response. "Oh, really? Did you spend some time there considering my offer?"

"I did." Adam nodded appreciatively before shifting to shake his head. "But although it was very generous, I'm afraid I'll have to decline."

Tyran grimaced indifferently as he shrugged his shoulders. It was a dramatic gesture of disappointment that his facial expression didn't reflect. "Too bad. Now I'm just going to have to kill you."

Adam stood tall and crossed his arms with a cocky smirk. "You can try."

Tyran moved first, swinging his arm around for a quick punch, but Adam ducked out of the way before shooting his body up and tackling Tyran straight into the air. Adam stopped about a hundred feet off the ground, yet Tyran's momentum carried him further into the sky.

Eventually regaining his balance, Tyran stopped as well and charged back at Adam with an extended fist. The stone-armored super soldier dodged the attack and followed up with a roundhouse kick that sent Tyran plummeting towards the city below.

A skyscraper eventually halted Tyran's free fall before collapsing down on top of him. Adam then flew over to the crash site and hovered above the wreckage, waiting for Tyran to emerge.

For nearly a minute, a few tumbling pieces of rubble were the only signs of movement within the ruins. As Adam continued to wait, a gust of wind rushed past him, carrying the cloud of dust through the street and scaring off a flock of birds by the park.

The sudden noise drew Adam's attention, and while he was distracted, Tyran busted through the building's remains to punch Adam in the jaw. The blow put a small crack in Adam's armor and sent him stumbling backwards. Adam quickly regained his bearings and engaged Tyran as he charged ahead for a follow up. Again, the two warriors threw several punches and kicks back and forth while carelessly flying through the air.

As the skirmish reached its peak, Tyran connected with a straight on punch that sent Adam falling towards the city. Tyran gave chase and grappled with Adam just a few stories above the street. Together, they pulled up just before hitting the ground and flew down the street locked as one before slamming into the side of a building.

The wrestling foes continued to struggle for the upper hand as they soared through the building's lobby and out the other side. Upon reaching the city's marina, Adam managed to break free from Tyran's hold and flew off towards the middle of the ocean.

"What are you running from?" Tyran yelled, pausing for a brief moment before following him.

Adam abruptly changed course by diving into the water and emerging a moment later underneath his pursuer. Bursting through the surface, Adam tackled Tyran straight into the air and then spun over his body, delivering a hard kick to his opponent's midsection. The blow sent Tyran plummeting towards a dense garden at the center of the city.

Rising up from the small crater he left in the dirt, Tyran surveyed the thick foliage around him and noticed a light ruffling in the trees that grabbed his attention. "I didn't take you for the hiding type, Adam."

"Says the man who fled across the world the first chance he got."

Tyran turned to the voice only to see a fireball racing towards him. Without time to properly block it, Tyran dove out of the way, allowing the ball of fire to instantly ignite the tree behind him.

In a matter of seconds, the brush was completely engulfed in a flame that rapidly spread from branch to branch. Before he knew what was happening, Tyran was surrounded on all sides by an intense inferno that was incinerating the entire garden around him.

Distracted by the wall of flames, Tyran heard a twig snap behind him and turned into a rocky fist that mashed him in the jaw. After stumbling back, Tyran regained his footing and lightly touched his lip, tasting the blood smeared across his fingers.

He then smiled and charged ahead, engaging Adam in another exchange of moves and countermoves while the ferocious flames continued to roar around them. The blaze started to close in, squeezing their battle like a vice, but neither fighter paid attention to the intense heat encircling their bodies.

Rearing back, Tyran threw a hard punch, but Adam quickly chopped the attack down and grabbed Tyran by the throat. While gasping for air, Tyran's feet slowly left the ground as Adam lifted him straight up. Desperately fighting to break free, Tyran clawed at his captor's rocky wrist, futilely trying to keep the jagged tips of Adam's craggy fingers from digging into his neck.

Uncaring of the fire that had now begun to consume them, Adam continued to tighten his grip around Tyran's throat while staring into his frenzied eyes. "It's strange, isn't it? To be so powerful and yet completely aware that you're about to die. But don't worry. You've already been to hell, so you should know it's not much hotter than this."

Struggling for every breath, Tyran tucked his legs into his chest and then shot them out into Adam's stone abdomen. He dropped Tyran immediately and stumbled back as small spider cracks spread throughout his armor. Now free, Tyran flew up and over the flames and smoke of the scorched garden as Adam quickly chased after him.

Flying through the city, Tyran randomly veered left and right, but no matter how fast he turned Adam was always gaining on him. Tyran stopped abruptly, ready to unleash a surprise attack, but Adam was nowhere to be found. Tyran looked around confused when Adam suddenly tackled him from behind.

Helpless in Adam's grasp, Tyran could see the ground fast approaching as the two of them plummeted downward at full speed. In a last, futile attempt to free himself, Tyran frantically grasped at Adam holding onto his back, but it was too late. He was slammed face first into the desolate street, forming a large, gaping crater in the center of downtown Tokyo.

Adam stood to his feet and gracefully floated up to stand at the crater's edge. Looking down into the hole, he saw Tyran wearily wobbling to his feet but still alive and ready for more.

Adam fired a quick blast at him, which Tyran evaded by flying high straight into the air. Adam followed after him but there wasn't a chase to be had. Too exhausted to run, Tyran stopped his flight several hundred feet above the ground and waited for Adam to catch up.

As the two super soldiers faced off it was clear who had the upper hand. While Adam's rocky armor had several chips and cracks throughout, it was nothing compared to Tyran's ripped and torn blood-drenched fatigues. He floated in the air hunched over while trying to catch his breath. It was a sight that made Adam smile before he charged again to resume their fight.

Tyran spent the entire bout on the defensive, using up all the energy he had left to deflect Adam's attacks, but it still wasn't enough. With each punch and kick, Adam came closer and closer to landing a strike.

Realizing the end was in sight, Tyran quickly flipped backwards and in one swift motion fired a desperate energy blast with the last of his power. Adam crossed his arms and blocked the concentrated wave, but Tyran didn't let up, holding onto the beam of energy in a stalemate. Grinding his teeth, Adam fought hard to keep from giving in, and Tyran did the same, screaming as loud as he could to push the blast through his opponent's shield.

When he felt the resistance to his attack give in, Tyran released the wave of energy and looked around, shocked that Adam was nowhere in sight. "I did it. He's gone."

"Not really."

Tyran's joyful expression suddenly faded as he looked up to discover Adam right beside him and about to unleash his own wave of energy. Unprepared to defend himself, Tyran took the blast hard and was shot like a missile towards the ground. He crashed hard into the street, forming another crater in the pavement. Although this one was significantly smaller than before, Tyran was not able to get out of it as his body collapsed upon his first attempt to stand.

Adam flew down and landed softly next to his beaten and bloody opponent. "It's over, Tyran. You've lost."

Looking up at Adam from the rubble that would be his deathbed, Tyran began to laugh hysterically. "Losing is only a matter of perspective."

"You find that funny?" asked Adam, annoyed by the show of humor.

Undeterred by globs of blood coughing out of his mouth, Tyran continued to chuckle. "I might've beaten you before, but I knew you'd come to play this time. So I wasn't taking any chances."

Confused by the vague response, Adam scrunched his face. "What does that mean?"

"It means I took the initiative and made sure we weren't the only ones with these powers in the new world."

"What are you talking about?" asked Adam, still confused by Tyran's revelation.

"You think you and I got this far by ourselves? We're just pawns, and when you failed to play your part I had to step up by sending copies of Groves's notes to every country looking to start their very own super soldier program."

Tyran continued to smile, basking in his final moment of glory, but Adam remained emotionless. "The procedure doesn't work for everyone, Tyran. You know that."

The smile finally relaxed, leaving only content satisfaction on Tyran's face. "The rules have changed, kid. It's only a matter of time before the Earth's overrun with super powered maniacs trying to take over the world. And there's nothing you can do about it."

Tyran laid back, surprised to feel so comfortable in the crushed cement beneath him. A moment later, Adam raised his arm and fired a short, contained blast that echoed through the barren streets. The energy wave completely immersed Tyran within it, disintegrating his entire body into fine points of ash.

Standing over the small, empty crater, Adam watched the tiny flakes that used to be Andrew Tyran drift up into the wind when a woman's throaty voice broke his concentration. "You don't feel any better, do you?"

Adam turned around and was unsurprised to see the old woman standing in the middle of the empty street.

"That's the funny thing about vengeance," she went on. "Revenge is nothing more than human emotion getting in the way of karma."

Adam remained still and showed zero emotion with his eyes and mouth, the only visible portions of his masked face. "I had a feeling you would show up sooner or later."

The feeble woman showed off a subtle, prideful smirk. "Of course you did. You were always a smart child."

Ignoring the compliment, Adam lowered his head disheartened and took a deep, sorrowful breath. "What Tyran said…is it true?"

"Yes."

"But why?" asked Adam, his gaze still trained on the ground. "I thought…"

His voice trailed off, hoping that the woman would be able to finish the sentence herself, but she snorted instead, practically mocking him. "You thought what? You were special? Chosen?"

The old woman laughed as Adam slowly looked up, shaking his head at the realization that just entered his mind. "You… used me."

The woman stopped laughing but her amused expression remained. "'Used' is such a harsh word. I like 'influenced' better."

"But why?" asked Adam, confused and insulted by the revelation. "Who are you?"

"It doesn't matter who I am," she said, shaking her head. "All that matters is what we…I have accomplished."

"Which is?"

The woman opened her arms, gesturing to the devastated city surrounding them. "A world of war."

Adam didn't understand. "That's all you wanted? War?" The frail woman lowered her arms, calmly clasping her hands in front of her. "My kind thrives on the pain, destruction, and suffering of civilizations. Achilles. Vlad the Impaler. Grigori Rasputin. We've been granting men some form of dominance to cause chaos and disarray since the day Cain first slew his brother. But we need more in this new world of extravagance and mania. We wanted to create a whole planet of misery and you, my crowning achievement, were going to help us."

Adam raised his stone hands and stared at them, struggling to accept the woman's manipulation. "Groves never gave me this power, did he? It was you all along."

The woman nodded softly. "The procedure I inspired him to design was nothing more than a catalyst. It allowed me to elevate your body into godhood in ways I could've never done on my own. Without my guidance, though, you would've perished like all his other subjects."

Adam's legs buckled under the immense weight of the truth and he collapsed to his knees as the woman continued to speak. "When I found you in New York you were lost. A futureless boy detached from the rest of humanity. A child with no cause and not a soul to care for him. So I gave you power. I gave you a purpose."

The old woman then hobbled over and knelt down beside him. "I gave you the opportunity to change the world, Adam, in a way like no one before you. You could've done anything and held the entire planet in the palm of your hand. But instead you deemed mankind too flawed to exist and went on some kind a self-righteous crusade to 'save' it from itself. How preposterous. I've known pharaohs with less hubris."

Languid and dejected, Adam looked up at the woman from his knees. "I thought you said you thrive on destruction. Isn't that what I was doing? Destroying humanity?"

"Yes. And it would've been quite enjoyable for the short term, but you were going to eradicate the entire species off the face of the Earth. What good are humans to me if there aren't any here to kill each other?"

The woman stood from kneeling and continued forward

past Adam, taking several more steps down the street. "So I needed a way to stop you."

"Tyran," said Adam, looking over his shoulder at her.

The woman spun on her heels to turn around and face him. "I thought maybe Andrew could change your mind and steer you back along the path I intended. However, when it became clear that wasn't going to happen I ordered him to share Dr. Groves's notes with every sovereign nation around the globe. Now, my kind will fill the whole world with super soldiers, all fighting and killing on the grandest scale imaginable."

Revitalized with a fury, Adam rose up and clenched his rocky fists at his sides. "I stopped Tyran. I will stop them, too."

"Yes," acknowledged the woman with a slow, lumbering nod. "Your power has grown far beyond anything I bestowed upon you. It's actually quite impressive. I was rather hoping Andrew would be able to stop this misguided quest of yours, but that didn't mean I wasn't prepared with a back up plan."

Although not necessarily concerned, Adam's curiosity had been piqued. "And what might that be?"

"I can't take all the credit for it," said the woman with a lofty smugness. "It was actually the final project Mr. Hopkins had been developing in the very facility where you were raised. I believe he called it the Fifth Horseman."

Adam became troubled, realizing he should've asked more questions when Hopkins was still alive. "He mentioned that name to me earlier."

The woman turned to her side and began pacing along the street as she explained. "It's an antimatter weapon. A bomb, essentially, with enough power to send half this island into oblivion. Hopkins had a dead man's switch implanted inside his heart, which you activated by killing him. As we speak an intercontinental ballistic missile carrying the device is headed this way, locked into its master's last known coordinates, and once it hits, I doubt even you can survive or outrun the blast."

Adam had many thoughts running through his head, but his anger and rage remained focused on only one thing: the one person standing before him. "And what about you? You'll die, too."

The woman stopped pacing and spoke to Adam with her shoulder turned to him. "Don't worry about me. I'm more resourceful than you could imagine."

In a sudden burst, Adam stormed the woman, ready to strike, but she quickly put out her hand, halting Adam's charge mid stride. Frozen still, he tried to move but found his muscles locked in position. The woman then closed her hand into a fist, squeezing an immense vice-like force around Adam's body. "Let's take this silly thing off and see that beautiful face of yours."

Adam let out a blood-curdling scream in pain as the layer of rock coating his body began to crack and the helmet covering his head instantly crushed into a hundred pieces.

"There. Isn't that better?" she asked, sarcastically.

The woman then opened her fist, releasing her hold on the super soldier and dropping him to his knees in front of her. "You looked like some kind of goofy super hero with that mask. But you're not a hero, Adam. No one is. We're all just villains trying to survive."

She continued to stand over him as he desperately tried to slow his rapidly, wheezing breaths. "Don't even try it. I created you and made sure you could never have enough power to—"

Adam abruptly lifted his hands off the ground and, from his knees, unleashed the strongest energy blast he had ever fired. Every ounce of life and willpower was put into a single, concentrated wave that engulfed the woman's body from point blank. He held onto the blast, fighting to push harder and inject more force into the attack.

Adam let out a horrific, agonizing scream as his entire body was drained of its power, and when he finally let go, all that remained was a strange, green skeleton that hung suspended in the air. A moment later, the bones dropped to the ground and spilled across the street the exact same time Adam collapsed from exhaustion.

Lying on his beck, Adam could hear the faint roar of a rocket echoing in the distance. As the thunderous sound grew intensely louder with every second, Adam didn't even bother to try and move, knowing his efforts would be pointless. He simply laughed and smiled to himself, content with the view he had staring up at the sky as the Fifth Horseman fell from the heavens.

# ABOUT THE AUTHOR

Frank Martin is an author and comic writer that is not as crazy as his work makes him out to be. A fan of storytelling in all its forms, Frank always enjoys exploring new genres and mediums. He currently lives in New York with his wife and three kids. You can check out updates for all of Frank's writing at frankthewriter.com, on his Facebook page at facebook.com/ frankmartinwriter, or follow him on Twitter and Instagram @ frankthewriter.

Published works:

*Modern Testament* (comics)
*Mountain Sickness*
*Predestiny (with C. T. Phipps)*

Curious about other Crossroad Press books?
Stop by our site:
http://store.crossroadpress.com
We offer quality writing
in digital, audio, and print formats.

Enter the code FIRSTBOOK
to get 20% off your first order from our store!
Stop by today!

www.ingramcontent.com/pod-product-compliance
Lightning Source LLC
Chambersburg PA
CBHW060432180626
46817CB00007B/2776